CAN ANYONE BE TRUSTED?

The locker area was quiet as Lisa entered. She quickly scooped up her things and headed for the door. As she was about to exit, she stopped short and turned back. Carole's cubby was open. Worse, her judging folder was sticking out where anybody could get to it! Lisa remembered how worried her friend had been that something might happen to the folder. Without another thought, Lisa moved quickly to the locker. She reached out to shove the items safely back inside when Carole tripped open the changing curtain, shouting, "Got you!"

Lisa was so startled she actually gave a small scream.

Carole stared, her face a mask of astonishment and anger. "You? You're the one who did it? All this time I've been racking my brains trying to figure out who had gotten into my folder, but it never occurred to me that it might have been Stevie or you!" Carole's voice was shaking and her eyes were full of tears. "I thought I knew you, but I don't know you at all!" With that, she ran out of the room, clutching her folder to her chest.

Other books you will enjoy

CAMY BAKER'S HOW TO BE POPULAR
IN THE SIXTH GRADE by Camy Baker

HORSE CRAZY (The Saddle Club #1) by Bonnie Bryant

AMY, NUMBER SEVEN (Replica #1) by Marilyn Kaye

PURSUING AMY (Replica #2) by Marilyn Kaye

ANASTASIA ON HER OWN by Lois Lowry

THE BOYS START THE WAR/
THE GIRLS GET EVEN by Phyllis Reynolds Naylor

the SADDLE CLUB

SHOW JUDGE

BONNIE BRYANT

A SKYLARK BOOK
NEW YORK • TORONTO • LONDON • SYDNEY • AUCKLAND

Special thanks to Sir "B" Farms
and Laura Roper

RL: 5, ages 009–012

SHOW JUDGE
A Bantam Skylark Book / November 2000

ISBN 0-553-48699-3

Visit us on the Web! www.randomhouse.com/kids
Educators and librarians, for a variety of teaching tools, visit us at
www.randomhouse.com/teachers

Published simultaneously in the United States and Canada

PRINTED IN THE UNITED STATES OF AMERICA
OPM   10 9 8 7 6 5 4 3 2 1

My special thanks to Cat Johnston for her help in the writing of this book.

"THIS IS REALLY great lasagna, Mr. Lake," Carole Hanson raved as she wiped her mouth with her napkin.

"Maybe the best ever," agreed Lisa Atwood.

"This is one of the bonuses when you guys spend the night," Stevie Lake chimed in. "My dad has to dig out this awesome recipe."

Stevie's father glowed with pleasure at the shower of compliments. "Mushrooms," he declared. "The secret is mushrooms!"

"Lasagna's the only good thing about having a bunch of girls sleeping over," grumbled Stevie's youngest brother.

"Michael, don't be rude," Mrs. Lake scolded. "It's always a pleasure having you girls stay with us."

"Mom's got a point," Chad muttered from across the table. "With the two of you to distract Miss Motormouth, the rest of us may actually get a chance to use the telephone."

Stevie glared at her brother. He might have been older, but there was no way she was going to let him get away with that comment. "Here's a quarter, Chad," she said, flicking a coin at him. "Why don't you call someone who might care?" The quarter landed closer to her twin brother Alex's plate. Faster than a rattlesnake, he snatched it off the table.

"Hey!" Stevie protested, holding out her hand for its return.

"Finders keepers!" He grinned at her in triumph.

"That's enough, you three," said Mrs. Lake. "Now, girls, what time is your Horse Wise meeting tomorrow?"

Horse Wise was the name of their Pony Club. They all looked forward to the regular meetings at Pine Hollow Stables.

"Mom," groaned Stevie. "It's been at the same time every Saturday for years."

"I think your mom was just testing you, sweetheart," her father teased.

2

Chad reached for some more buttery garlic bread. "It's a good thing that test was about horses, otherwise she'd have had zero chance of passing it."

"At least I know something about something," Stevie replied tartly. "Even with all the riding lessons you've taken, I could still write what you know about horses on the head of a pin!"

"Chad is a pinhead, Chad is a pinhead," Michael began to chant.

"Oh, shut up!" said Chad, pinging him with a small bread ball from across the table.

Michael ducked. "You shut up!"

"No, you shut up!"

Michael had an amazing ability to bring older kids down to his own level.

Carole and Lisa watched and listened in stunned silence. Neither one of them could ever recall a scene remotely like this taking place in her own home.

Carole lived with her widowed father, who was a Marine Corps colonel, and although he was a lot of fun and loved to share silly jokes, there was no way he would put up with this kind of behavior at the table.

As for Lisa, she knew the very idea of raising her voice at dinner would upset her mother, who was a stickler for good manners at all times. Even if her older brother had been around more often, she couldn't imagine the two of them behaving like this.

"Chad! We do not throw food at the table," his mother chastised him. "Now, don't you have something to say to your brother?"

Chad lowered his head. "All right. I'm sorry I dinged you with a bread ball."

"And I'm sorry you didn't use something heavier," cracked Alex. Stevie and her twin brother laughed and high-fived each other.

Their father ran a hand through his hair. "Settle down, kids. By the way, someone left the back door open again."

Chad looked up with the face of pure innocence. "That was Stevie—as usual." He returned to scarfing his food.

Stevie ignored the comment and rested her chin on one hand. "What happened today, Chad? Didn't like your packed lunch?"

He stopped eating. "How did you know—Hey! So that was you?" He rose partially to his feet. "I should have known!"

"Chad, sit down!" His mother pointed a finger at him. "Didn't you like your meat loaf sandwich?"

Chad lowered himself back into his chair but his eyes never left his sister. "I didn't get a meat loaf sandwich, Mom. Did I, Stevie?"

Lisa could tell from Stevie's face that her friend had just been caught in her own net. Stevie was known for her practical jokes, which were as irresistible to her as catnip is to a cat, and she and Chad were particularly ruthless with one another.

Mrs. Lake's gaze shifted to her daughter. "All right, Stevie, what did Chad get for lunch?"

Silence.

"Stevie?" her father said with authority.

Stevie looked sheepish. "Sardines on rye bread."

"Come on, keep it coming," prodded Chad.

"Okay, okay." She broke. "Sardines on rye with sauerkraut, pickles, and ketchup."

"Ew!" squealed Michael.

"But I did leave him a nice cream soda to wash it down with," Stevie added in her own defense.

"Oh man, Dad!" cried Chad. "I took a big bite of it and almost puked!"

"Well, it serves you right, you creepoid!" Stevie turned to her two friends. "Last week he poured water into Madonna's kitty litter box and the clay stuck to her paws. She practically had cement boots when that stuff hardened!"

Alex began to snicker. "Man, that was a good one."

"Yeah, a good one," mimicked Michael.

"You two just shut up," Stevie practically yelled at them. "Remember, you're not immune, either."

Alex bristled. "Oh yeah? You just try something and see what comes your way!"

"Yeah, we're not scared of you!"

With that, pandemonium broke out at the table, with all the kids yelling at once.

Mr. Lake slammed his hand down on the table hard enough to make the glasses and silverware jump. "Enough!" he shouted. "That is enough!"

"Absolutely," their mother added, rising to her feet and throwing down her napkin. "You've reduced this house to complete chaos with your bickering. Your father and I want some peace and quiet for a change! Is that too much to ask?"

Silence.

"Well, is it?" she demanded, eyeballing her children. Stevie, Chad, Alex, and Michael all hung their heads in shame. "No, Mom," they mumbled together.

Mr. Lake turned to Lisa and Carole. "I'm sorry you girls had to see this. I'd like to think tonight's behavior is the exception, not the rule, for this house." He shifted his angry gaze to the Lake children. "Under the circumstances, I think everybody should just be excused."

Stevie was totally embarrassed. She had rarely seen her father so angry, and he'd certainly never lost his temper in front of company before. "Mom, Dad, I'm sorry," she said.

"Don't you think you owe Chad an apology as well?" her mother asked, still frowning.

Stevie was unable to think of a way out, but she refused to look her brother in the eye as she did it. "I'm sorry about your sandwich, Chad."

"I'm sorry about your cat," he muttered, focusing on his plate. "I guess," he added.

"I believe it's your turn, Alex," Mr. Lake prodded.

"I'm sorry about the crack about using something heavier, Michael," Alex said, sounding anything but.

Mr. and Mrs. Lake looked at their youngest son expectantly.

"But I didn't do anything!" he complained.

Mr. Lake's frown deepened.

7

Michael joined his siblings in lowering his eyes to the table. "I'm sorry," he said to no one in particular.

Eager to make some kind of amends, Stevie offered to take care of the dishes. Lisa and Carole immediately volunteered to help. As they cleaned up, the three girls talked quietly among themselves. "So, Stevie," Carole asked, "what's up with you and your brothers?"

"Yeah, I've heard of sibling rivalry, but that was something else," added Lisa, her head still swimming.

Stevie loaded the dishwasher. "I don't know. They've really been getting on my nerves lately."

"You wouldn't play any practical jokes on Michael," said Carole, "would you?"

Stevie smiled wickedly. "No, of course not, but wouldn't it be funny if he came in one day and found sardine skeletons floating in the bowl?"

Stevie couldn't help giggling at the picture. Her friends didn't find it quite so funny.

"So . . . ," Stevie said, shutting the dishwasher door and hitting the Start button. "Are we done here? Because if we are, may I suggest we call a meeting of The Saddle Club?"

The Saddle Club, a club the three girls had formed,

had only two rules: one, you had to be absolutely horse-crazy, and two, you had to be willing to help the other members out, no matter what. Since they were all head over heels about horses and the best of friends, the rules were easy to follow. Of course from time to time Stevie's practical jokes landed her in hot water, leaving her two pals to bail her out. They didn't mind, though, because she had a good and fun-loving heart, and even though she came from a well-off family, she never put on any airs or graces like some other people—namely, her arch rival at the stable, the snobby Veronica diAngelo.

Lisa was the least experienced rider of the three, but she was progressing very quickly, and her friends and riding instructors said she had natural ability. She was definitely the most levelheaded of the group, although she tended to put a lot of pressure on herself to over-achieve. Stevie and Carole were helping her learn to lighten up and have fun.

Although one grade behind Lisa, Carole was the most experienced horsewoman. After her mother died of cancer, her dad encouraged her riding by buying a horse, which Carole named Starlight. She knew one thing for certain: whatever she decided to be in life, it was definitely going to have to do with horses. The possibilities included becoming a veterinarian, owning and breeding horses, and maybe being a professional rider.

Once safely behind the locked door of Stevie's bedroom, the girls' talk quickly turned to the upcoming Horse Wise meeting at Pine Hollow Stables. At their last meeting, the owner of the stables, Maxmillian Regnery III—whom everybody just called Max—had hinted at a very special upcoming project, and the girls were dying to find out what it was.

"I suppose it could be another guest lecturer," Lisa speculated.

"How about another overnight trail ride?" suggested Stevie. "I love those."

Carole threw a pillow at her. "That's because Phil sometimes gets to come along."

Stevie's boyfriend, Phil Marsten, lived out of town, so he and Stevie only got to see each other once or twice a month, but they talked on the phone often. They were both horse-crazy.

Stevie laughed, ducking her friend's fluffy missile. "So what's your point?"

Before Carole could answer there was a knock on the door. She started to get up to open it, but Stevie launched herself across the room, blocking the way.

"Don't open it! Don't even make any noise!" She pulled her two friends toward the closet, whispering urgently in their ears. "Brothers! Revenge! Retribution! We've got to hide!"

She yanked open the door and a knee-deep mound of very horsey-smelling laundry fell out. Lisa backed away, waving a hand under her nose. "Phew, I'm not going in there!"

"Stevie, open up!" Chad called through the door. He sounded annoyed.

"Quick, under the bed!" cried Stevie.

Carole dropped to her knees, lifted the ruffle, and stopped dead.

"What's the matter?" asked Stevie.

"Have you looked under here lately?"

"What about it?"

"Do you remember all those things that disappeared in the Bermuda Triangle? I think I just found them."

"Oh, come on, it's not that bad."

Carole gave her a look, reached under the ruffle, and pulled out a pair of pajama bottoms covered in dust bunnies. That was followed by an old hairbrush, a yo-yo with no string, a few mismatched socks, and a stuffed blue dog coated nose to tail in lint and dust.

Stevie unhesitatingly grabbed the plush toy and hugged it. "Wubbie! There you are!"

"What's this?" asked Carole, studying the last object she'd extracted. "Your history report?"

"Hey, I've been looking for that all over the place."

"When exactly was it due?" Lisa asked.

"Actually, a week ago. But it's okay, I told my teacher the dog ate it."

"Stevie, you don't have a dog," Carole reminded her.

Stevie held up the stuffed hound dog with a grin.

Lisa shook her head, chuckling. "Sometimes I just don't believe you."

"It's not like I didn't do the work," Stevie said sulkily.

Pounding rattled the door. Stevie figured that outside of jumping through the window and sliding down the drainpipe, there was no avenue of escape. She had seriously considered the possibility, but they were already in their nightgowns and it might prove undignified. She opened the door.

All three brothers stood there.

"About time," Alex griped.

12

Stevie braced herself for a possible water balloon attack but nothing happened.

"Can we talk to you?" Chad asked.

"I can't say I've seen any evidence of talking so far tonight," whispered Lisa to Carole. They both giggled.

"All right, come in. But no funny business."

"Truce."

The boys walked in. "Look, we guys got talking, and I think I've figured out why Mom and Dad came unglued tonight," Chad said. "They've got a major anniversary coming up in two weeks."

"That's right!" cried Stevie. "I totally forgot."

Her parent's twentieth wedding anniversary. How could she have forgotten such an important event? She had a hard enough time just imagining herself ever being twenty, let alone being married for twenty years. "We've got to get them something spectacular!"

"That's what we thought, too," agreed Chad.

"Then Alex suggested—"

"And me!" Michael cried, pushing forward, not wanting to be left out.

"And Michael," amended Chad. "They suggested that if we all pooled our money, maybe we could come up with something really cool, instead of just four average presents."

"That's not a bad idea," Carole said from the bed.

"Not bad at all," added Lisa.

"But what can we get them?" Stevie asked.

"What about one of those Caribbean cruises?" suggested Alex. "I've seen Mom watch the commercials and get all dreamy-eyed."

"I don't know how much money you guys have, but I don't think we can quite swing that," Stevie said reluctantly.

Michael started jumping up and down. "We could get a new whatchamacallit for the swimming pool."

"He means a new pump," Stevie explained to her friends. "The old one broke. And that's a good idea, Mike, but not very romantic for Mom and Dad. I think whatever it is should be about them, not us. Don't you?" Michael nodded and Stevie patted him on the head. "What about dance lessons?"

Chad shot the suggestion down quickly. "That's okay for Mom, but Dad . . ." He and his brothers made faces. "A membership at the gym?"

"They'd never have time to use it," Alex said.

"You're probably right," Chad agreed. "Maybe season passes to the hockey games?"

It was Stevie's turn to make a face. "Oh, Mom would love that!" she said sarcastically.

"A puppy?" Michael suggested excitedly.

Chad gave him a wry smile. "Sorry, sport. Nice try, though."

"Tickets to the ballet in Washington?"

"Yuck."

"Jet Skis?"

"Where would they use them?"

"Matching sets of golf clubs?"

"We could barely afford covers for their old ones."

The ideas came fast and furious, but none of them seemed quite right or within their financial reach. It was something of a relief when their parents called up to say it was time for bed. They decided to sleep on it and talk about it more the next day.

That left more time for Stevie, Carole, and Lisa to talk about their upcoming meeting.

"So, what do you suppose Max is up to?" Lisa asked. "He was so mysterious!"

"Jet Skis!" Stevie said. Her mind was obviously still on the conversation with her brothers.

The girls fell into a sleepy silence in the dark of Stevie's room. The last conscious thought that danced through Stevie's head was a vision of her parents standing in front of the house as she presented them with a giant pair of scissors to cut the huge red ribbon off their brand-new shiny Mercedes convertible. Her brothers, of course, were nowhere to be seen.

2

SATURDAY MORNING WAS bright and beautiful. The Saddle Club actually managed to arrive a little early, in spite of Stevie's being her usual disorganized self.

Since Max had announced at the previous meeting that that day was going to be a mounted gathering, the stable was a beehive of activity. At the moment almost all the riders were in a frenzy of last-minute checks on their horses' grooming and tack. Max was a wonderful riding teacher, and a part of what made him really good was that he cared. He could joke with the young riders about all kinds of things—except horses. When it came to riding and horse care, he was all business. He frowned severely on riders who were late or whose horses were carelessly turned out.

"I've got Starlight ready to go, Stevie," called Carole. "Do you need any help?"

"I think I'm ready, too. Have you checked on Lisa?"

"She's helping one of the younger kids." Carole watched as Stevie finished up. "Wow, you're actually ready early. I think you may be setting a dangerous precedent here. Personally I'd never have believed it was possible. Especially today."

"Why?"

"Have you forgotten that frantic search for your favorite pair of jeans this morning?"

"I told you everything was under control," Stevie said loftily.

"In other words, you were lying."

"There's no need to be vulgar. I have supreme confidence in my ability to arrive on time."

"Liar, liar, pants on fire," Carole chanted.

"I refuse to sink to your level," Stevie said, leading Belle out of her stall. "Come on, you can walk me out."

Carole gave a gentle tug on Starlight's reins, falling into step beside her friend. "This is such an honor."

"Oh, be quiet," Stevie giggled, bumping her friend's shoulder with her own.

They were both still ribbing each other when they emerged from the stable. Veronica diAngelo was outside, brushing a nonexistent piece of lint off her tailored jacket, completely self-absorbed, as usual. A couple of steps away, Corey Takamura sat on her pony, Samurai, struggling with one of her stirrups. "Excuse me, Veronica," she asked shyly. "I think there's something wrong with my stirrup. Could you please help me?"

The look Veronica shot her would have chilled an ice cube. "I can't believe how selfish you are, Corey," she snapped, pulling a pair of riding gloves from her pocket and putting them on. "See these gloves? They're made of the finest kid. Do you actually expect me to drop everything, walk all the way over there, and let you put your dirty old boots all over them?"

Stevie turned to Carole and rolled her eyes. "Did you hear her? She'd have to take two, maybe three steps tops"—she put on her best Veronica imitation—"to come all the way over there."

"Not to mention the fact that she wasn't wearing her gloves when Corey asked for help," fumed Carole. "She just put them on so she'd have a better reason not to do anything."

19

Veronica apparently hadn't finished with poor Corey. "If you paid better attention in class in the first place, you'd know how to fix it yourself. Maybe you're wasting Max's time being here."

Even from the barn doorway the girls could see Corey crumbling with humiliation.

"If you really can't figure out such a simple thing like how to adjust your own stirrup," continued Veronica, "I suggest you find Red O'Malley. That's what stable hands are for."

That was the last straw for Stevie. She sauntered casually forward with Belle in tow. "Veronica, it looks like I owe you an apology."

Veronica greeted her with cool, suspicious eyes. "What for?"

"I always thought you had Red tack up your horse for you because you were lazy. But if I just heard you right, it's because you don't know how to do it yourself," Stevie said. "You did tell Corey, 'If you can't figure out how to do a simple thing, call for the stable hand,' didn't you?"

Veronica raised her chin haughtily. "I use Red for the tasks for which he is employed."

"I don't think *doormat* is written in his job description," Stevie replied wryly.

Veronica glared at her and stalked away, brushing past Lisa, who had just arrived leading Prancer.

"Uh-oh! What was that about?" Lisa wanted to know.

Stevie just grinned and went to help Corey with her stirrup.

"Veronica was being her usual nasty self," Carole explained. "Stevie took her down a peg or two."

"Oh dear," Lisa said, swinging easily into the saddle. She felt it was never a good idea to embarrass Veronica diAngelo, whose family was the richest in town and, in fact, held the mortgage on Pine Hollow. Veronica and Stevie had been butting heads for a long time now and so far Stevie had come out on top, but with Veronica you could never be sure how or when she might choose to get her revenge. "I hope that doesn't come back to haunt us."

Carole also mounted up. "Sooner or later you know it will."

"Well, I'm hoping for later rather than sooner," said Lisa. "Hey, Stevie, Corey, let's go. Max is ready to begin."

Stevie climbed on Belle and joined them, and they rode over to meet the rest of the class assembled outside the ring.

Max gave all the riders and horses a once-over, making adjustments here and there and handing out occasional words of advice. Finally he came to Veronica's horse, Danny, and eyed the Thoroughbred's glossy coat. "I have to say, Danny is looking wonderfully groomed as usual, Veronica, and your tack has obviously been extremely well cleaned and cared for."

Veronica gave him an ingratiating, self-congratulatory smile. "Thank you."

"I must remember to commend Red on his good work."

Veronica's face fell. Every rider there knew that she made Red do as many of her chores as she possibly could, and Max was letting her know that she was fooling no one, least of all him.

"All right then," he continued briskly. "I'm going to pair you all up, one senior rider with one beginner rider. When I call out your name, please move over next to your partner. The idea here is for the more knowledgeable students to try their hand at coaching. I think this will be a mutual learning experience for all."

Stevie was delighted at the possibilities. She had so much good advice to pass on that she hardly knew where to start! She was just as happy when her partner turned out to be Corey, and Corey seemed equally pleased by the pairing. After all, Corey and two of her friends Jasmine James and May Grover so admired The Saddle Club that they had formed their own version of it, which they called the Pony Tails.

"Lisa," called Max. "You'll work with Jasmine."

Lisa felt her heart sink and her stomach clench at the announcement. It wasn't that she didn't like Jasmine; on the contrary, she liked her a lot. Assuming responsibility for her schooling, however, made Lisa shake inside. What if she blew it? What if she didn't know the answer to Jasmine's questions, or, even worse, taught her the wrong answers? Lisa knew she had a natural talent for riding, but she also knew she was relatively new to the sport.

Almost as if she sensed her friend's distress, Carole moved her horse up close to the new pair and smiled. "Jasmine, I hope you realize you've got one of the best partners in the group. Years of ballet have given Lisa really good balance, which means she's got an excellent seat. Maybe she'll share some of her secrets with you."

"Would you, Lisa?" Jasmine enthused. "That would be great! I could really use some help on that."

"I'd be happy to help you," Lisa said, her confidence

23

lifted by her friend's praise. She smiled gratefully at Carole.

Max was finishing up the assignments. "Okay, that should take care of it."

Carole looked around, confused. Max must have made some kind of mistake: She didn't have a partner, but everyone else seemed to. Crestfallen, she realized she was the only rider left.

Lisa must have seen the disappointment on her face. "Hey, Max, what about Carole? She didn't get a partner."

"Don't worry, Lisa, I have something special in mind for her."

That immediately got everyone's attention. Especially Carole's.

He walked over and put a hand on Starlight's neck, stroking the animal gently. The horse turned to snuffle him affectionately. "I want you all to think of the person you're paired with as your Pony Partner. As our most experienced and accomplished rider, Carole is going to be *everyone's* Pony Partner. That means as you work with your partners, the two of us will be available to help you with any problems or questions you may have."

Carole felt herself swell with pride. The fact that Max had such confidence in her skill and knowledge was a real pat on the back.

"Let's get to work," he ordered.

With that, the pairs all headed in different directions. Lisa gave Carole a grin and a big thumbs-up. Jasmine mimicked the gesture.

Stevie rode up with Corey in tow. "Poor May," she said, shaking her head sadly.

Carole had been caught up in her thoughts and didn't follow. "What's wrong with May?"

Stevie directed a mournful gaze toward the eight-year-old rider sitting on her shaggy yellow pony, Macaroni. "Notice who she got paired up with?"

"Veronica," Lisa said with sympathy. "They say if you do a bad thing in a previous life, you have to pay for it in this one."

"Are you saying that May was a tyrant in her last incarnation?" laughed Carole.

Corey and Jasmine appeared a little confused by the conversation, but the other three girls had to laugh. May, whose father was a professional trainer, was one of the most talented of the young riders. She could be a bit bossy at times, but she definitely didn't deserve Veronica for a Pony Partner.

"Well, someone had to get Veronica," said Stevie. "Maybe Carole, our second in command, can keep a special eye on her."

"I think I might just do that," said Carole. "Good

25

luck, you two." They all parted company to begin their lessons.

The rest of the morning passed in a flurry of activity. Lisa set up a series of evenly spaced ground poles, demonstrating to Jasmine the technique of riding over them without using stirrups. The exercise was designed to enhance balance and encourage an independent seat in the rider. "Remember, Jasmine, stirrups are just an aid," she tutored. "Useful, absolutely, but a really good rider should be so balanced in the saddle that she can jump a fence without using them."

Carole strode up to the fence and watched Jasmine work. "How's she doing?"

Lisa made a so-so motion with her hand, without taking her eyes off her charge. "Try to keep your calves even with the saddle girth," she shouted to Jasmine.

"This work will really pay off when she starts working over raised cavalletti," Carole said knowingly. "It was a good choice of exercise for her, Lisa."

As Carole moved off to help someone else, Lisa smiled with pleasure, then turned her attention back to Jasmine.

IN ONE OF the pastures, Stevie was using her knowledge of dressage to help Corey work on her leg cues.

26

The two girls had just finished doing serpentines in tandem at the trot. Having drawn to a halt, Stevie was trying to explain the next part of the exercise to her Pony Partner. "It's really easy for a rider to become dependent on the reins for guiding her horse, but in dressage it's actually the legs that control most of the horse's movements." She was gratified to see how focused Corey was on every word she was saying. "When used correctly to apply pressure in different spots, along with little shifts of your body weight, you can tell your horse exactly what you want him to do, while using your reins hardly at all. Now, are you ready to give it a try?"

"I don't know," Corey said hesitantly. "What do you want me to do?"

"Exactly what we've been doing, but this time I want you to drop your reins and just use your legs to steer Samurai around the turns."

The young rider looked doubtful and a little scared. "What if he spooks and bolts?"

"Don't worry, I'll be right beside you the whole time," Stevie reassured her. "I won't let anything happen to you."

Corey smiled with more confidence, placed her reins carefully on her pony's neck, and together they broke into a trot.

27

* * *

CAROLE FOUND HERSELF almost run off her feet helping the other riders. She couldn't count on both hands the number of times she had had to call out to the various riders, "Head up and heels down!" She'd spent time explaining why stirrups that were the right length for riding were too long for jumping, how to judge the proper spacing for trotting poles, and that the proper height for cavalletti depended on the exercise they were being used for. At the end of the hour she felt both exhilarated and exhausted.

The only dark cloud in her day had come while she watched May schooling herself. Veronica, who should have been helping the girl, spent most of the time under a shade tree, reapplying her nail polish. Carole made it a point to give May a few bits of advice and encouragement, but it was frustrating to see the girl being ignored by the person who was supposed to be teaching her. She was tempted to tell Veronica off, but she didn't really want to get in an argument. Besides, May was Veronica's responsibility, not hers. Fortunately May was a talented rider, and Mac was a steady, hardworking pony. All in all they seemed to be managing fairly well by themselves.

When Max finally called a halt to the lesson, there was a general air of satisfaction and camaraderie about the group.

"Okay, I want you all to see to your horses, then meet me in the office," he told them. "There's something important I have to tell you, so don't chitchat the time away."

3

ONLY WHEN ALL the horses and ponies had been cooled down and put away and the last of the tack had been cleaned and hung in the tack room did the entire group assemble in Max's office. There was a good feeling in the air, a sense of satisfaction for work well done.

Max cleared his throat and the room fell silent. "I want you to know that I was very pleased with everyone today. I was especially happy to see all the pairs working so well together."

Many Pony Partners exchanged smiles.

"It was important for me to see just how well you worked together, because over the next two weeks you are going to spend a lot more time with each other. As some of you may already know, there is an under-twelve Pony Club rally coming up in four weeks. As always, I want my riders to be as well prepared as possible."

Carole, Stevie, and Lisa shared looks. They had heard this speech before. Max was known far and wide as a stickler for preparation. Both his riders and other professionals in the industry admired him for this discipline, which he imposed on himself as well as his students.

"Some of you have competed before; for others this will be your first time out. In either case"—he eyed the younger riders sternly—"you have a lot to learn before the meet. There's a lot more that goes into getting ready for a competition than simply riding skills. Carole, can you tell them what I'm talking about?"

Although startled by the question, Carole knew exactly the kinds of things he was referring to. "There's the care and preparation that goes into horse and rider to make sure they're both in peak condition physically and mentally on the day of the competition. The horses will need special diets to compensate for the extra time they'll have to put in. Of course, the more you ride, the more your tack will need to be carefully maintained, not to mention an extra-special cleaning the day before the show." She paused to collect her thoughts. "You'll need to make detailed lists of necessary items, including spare parts in case of emergencies, grooming kits, and, of course, food for your horses."

"Very good, Carole. I don't think I could have said it better myself."

Carole flushed with pride.

"Each of you deserves my individual attention, but there's only so much of me to go around, so I'm assigning each of you your own personal coaches. For the next two weeks the Pony Partner you worked with today will be your guide and adviser. At the end of that time you under-twelves will compete in our very own Horse Wise Show Skills Rally.

A murmur of excitement and speculation spread through the room.

Lisa turned to Stevie with dismay. "We're going to teach them to get ready for a show in only two weeks?"

"Isn't it great?" enthused Stevie.

"Excuse me, Max!" Veronica diAngelo's voice cut through the noise of the room. "What about Carole? She doesn't have a Pony Partner. It hardly seems fair to her; she'll have nothing to do at all."

"What she really means," whispered Stevie, "is that it's not fair that Carole doesn't have to work while *she* does."

"Since I've already had a chance to work with May today," continued Veronica sweetly, "maybe Carole would like to take over. I wouldn't want her to miss out on such a wonderful experience."

Max smiled. "That's very generous of you, Veronica. I know just how much this experience means to you, so I wouldn't have you miss it for the world."

It was all The Saddle Club could do not to howl with laughter. Max had known exactly what Veronica was up to. There was no way for her to squirm out now.

"Still, you have a point about Carole," he continued. "There is no reason why she should have to be the odd man out, so I am hereby appointing her as our official judge."

At that the room really did buzz with excitement.

"She will be observing the young riders throughout the next two weeks, and especially at our show. She'll be judging based on skills and growth on everything from grooming to jumping."

"Way to go, Carole!" squealed Stevie, patting her on the back."

"This is awesome," agreed Lisa, beaming at her friend.

Carole found herself speechless. All she could do was shake her head and smile.

Stevie nudged them both in the ribs. "Hey, did you catch the look on Veronica's face when Max made the announcement?"

"Absolutely priceless," confirmed Lisa, grinning.

"She looked like she ate something that didn't agree with her," chuckled Stevie.

"A chunk of pride, perhaps?" suggested Lisa.

Max quieted them down and continued. "No matter who Carole decides the winner is, I expect to see you *all* improve your skills over the next two weeks. If you can do that, I know you'll make me proud at the under-twelve rally, whether you win ribbons or not."

That seemed to signify the end of class, and they all rose to leave.

"Carole," Max called across the fast emptying room. "Can you come over here for a minute?"

"Sure, Max, be right there." She turned to Stevie and Lisa. "You two go ahead. I'll meet you in the locker room." She hurried over to Max.

"I have some things here you're going to need for the judging." He handed her a large file folder and a clipboard.

"Max, I want to thank you for letting me do this." Suddenly she felt tongue-tied. "I—I just want you to know, I won't let you down."

34

"Don't thank me yet, Carole," he said, giving her a solemn look. "No matter what Veronica may be thinking, this job is twice as difficult as any other, and you may regret taking it on before you're through."

Worried that he might be having second thoughts about her ability to carry out the assignment, Carole hurried to reassure him. "I know it's going to be hard work, but I think I'm up to it and I promise to be completely impartial."

"I'd expect nothing less from you," he said with a smile. "Now, I think you better get started. After all, you're on the clock starting right now, and who knows what your charges are up to?" With that he strode away like a man with a mission.

Before she got to work, Carole took a moment to see what the file folder contained. Attached to the top of the clipboard by a long string was a pencil. She smiled. Leave it to Max to make sure she would never be without a writing instrument. Inside the folder she found multiple copies of judging forms, one for each person in the group. They were divided into categories: horse care, tack care, attitude, appearance, and so on. Across from each category was a row of grading boxes ranging from ten to one. There was also a small pad for making notes and keeping records.

Carole hugged the items to her chest and took a deep, satisfied breath. She realized it was just a clipboard and some papers, but somehow it all made her feel very official. She was determined not to let anyone down. She would make The Saddle Club proud.

STEVIE AND LISA were sitting on benches in the locker room. "Well it's about time," Lisa said as Carole hurried in.

"Sorry," Carole said. "Official business."

"Ooooh, listen to Madame Judge," teased Stevie.

"What did Max say?" Lisa asked.

"That it's going to be harder work than I think. Considering all the paperwork he handed me, he may be right."

"What have you got there?" Lisa eyed her folder curiously.

Carole moved the papers out of reach. "Sorry, Lisa, for my eyes only. At least for the next two weeks," she added apologetically.

Lisa looked disappointed. "I've always wanted to see what a judging sheet looked like."

"Me too," Stevie sighed wistfully. "Every time I compete at a show and a judge scribbles something on one of those pieces of paper, I want to see what they're writing."

"I know how you feel," agreed Carole. "I've always been curious about it, too. Tell you what, when the competition is over we'll all sit down and go over my notes together."

"I guess then we'll find out what Carole really thinks about our riding and teaching skills, won't we, Lisa?"

"I can hardly wait," Lisa answered somewhat glumly.

Seeing her friend's worried face and knowing how insecure Lisa could be about her riding, Carole tried to lift her spirits and reassure her. "Oh come on, you guys, you already know what I think. You're both light-years ahead of the competition."

"How very interesting," came a chilly voice from the doorway. To Carole's dismay, Veronica and her pal Betsy Cavanaugh had just come in the room. "I guess we might as well withdraw from the competition right now," said Betsy. "Don't you think?"

"I'm sure you're right," snipped Veronica. "As May's trainer, how could I in good conscience let her compete for third place?" She eyed The Saddle Club trio with malice. "It's obvious first and second have already been decided."

"That's not fair," said Carole, coming to her feet.

"That was what you were implying, though, wasn't it? You did say Stevie and Lisa were better than all the rest of us."

"I—I didn't mean it that way," stammered Carole.

"That's what you say, but I wonder how everybody else will see it?" She turned to leave. "Come on, Betsy, we might as well break the bad news to the others."

At the sound of their retreating footsteps, Carole sank on to the bench and covered her face with her hands, groaning.

"Hey, Carole, it's okay," said Lisa. "It's just Veronica. Who cares what she thinks?"

"Yeah," agreed Stevie. "We know you would never play favorites, and so does everyone else in the stable. That's one of the reasons Max picked you."

Carole was grateful for her friends' loyalty, but the thought of Veronica and Betsy running around blabbing to everyone what she had said filled her with dismay. Maybe she should resign the judging position.

Stevie knelt in front of her. "You're going to be the best judge ever. Veronica is jealous and will do anything to make you look bad, you know that."

"Yeah," agreed Lisa. "But she's going to have to work a lot harder than this to do it."

"And we all know how Veronica feels about hard work!" laughed Stevie.

Carole mustered a weak smile.

"Hey," said Lisa, jumping to her feet. "I promised Jasmine I would show her some of the finer points of mucking out a stall. I gotta get moving."

"I didn't realize there were finer points to shoveling horse manure," Carole said.

"Then you'll just have to stop by and see a professional at work," Lisa answered grandly.

"Corey needs me, too," said Stevie, moving toward the door. "After all, I do hold the fate of the finest equestrienne in the world in the palm of my hand." She paused for a moment. "How about a Saddle Club meeting at TD's later?" TD's was their name for the Tastee Delight Ice Cream Parlor, the site of many of their get-togethers.

"Sounds great," said Lisa.

"Count me in," said Carole, pulling herself together.

With that, the others left her alone. Her thoughts returned to the scene with Veronica. How could she have been so careless? She'd have to be more cautious in the future, watch every move and word, so that absolutely no one, including Veronica diAngelo, could accuse her of being the least bit biased toward her friends or against anyone else.

39

Right then, however, the best thing for her to do was to get to work and see what was going on around the stable. She took a moment to organize her grading papers and left the locker area. As she made her rounds she found herself trying to be as inconspicuous as possible, still self-conscious about what Veronica and Betsy might have told everybody. She got a few sharp looks but in general everyone seemed too busy to pay much attention to her. Or were they ignoring her intentionally?

This is ridiculous, she finally told herself. *I have a job to do and I'm not going to get it done this way.* She moved on with new purpose. Rounding a corner, she was in time to watch Stevie instructing Corey on the best way to use a hoof pick. She leaned against the stall door to better observe the procedure.

". . . and when you're sure it's all clean and healthy, you gently put his foot back on the floor and give him a pat on the neck to tell him how good a pony he's been."

"I think you covered all the important points, Stevie," Carole said, as she scribbled on her notepad. "I know you've been cleaning hooves forever, but Corey may want to run her hand down Samurai's leg a little slower, to signal him that she wants to pick up his foot. That would help to build up his trust."

40

Stevie seemed to consider her words, then nodded thoughtfully. "You may be right. Belle and I are so used to each other, she almost seems to know what I want before I ask her. I forgot Corey and Samurai might still have some bonding to do. Thanks for the reminder."

"No problem." She almost added, *You guys are going to do great*, then thought better of it. "See you later."

Not long after, she came across Lisa and Jasmine, who were getting ready to feed Outlaw. "Stable horses like eating," Lisa was saying, "not only because it tastes good, but it breaks up the boredom of having to stand around most of the day. But remember, he needs to be watered a full half hour before you give him his oats."

"It smells good, don't you think?" Jasmine said, taking a deep whiff of the mixture of molasses, corn, and oats in the bucket she was holding. "Have you ever tasted it?"

"Oh sure, once or twice," Lisa assured her. "Want to try?"

Jasmine took a tentative taste. "Ewww!" she cried, spitting it out.

Lisa couldn't help laughing at the face the girl was making. "That's exactly how I felt about it, too," she said between giggles.

Jasmine also started laughing. "You did that on purpose!" she accused. "Why didn't you warn me?"

Lisa shrugged. "Some things you have to learn for yourself. Besides, sooner or later every rider tries it."

Jasmine had started to pour the bucket into the feed bin when Carole stepped forward. "Don't forget, Lisa, it's not good to feed an animal too much after a lot of exercise. Four times a day is best because horses have a small digestive capacity."

Lisa looked up, frowning a little. "I think I already mentioned that to Jasmine."

"Did you remember to mix some chaff in?" Carole asked, peering into the feed bin, then scribbling away in her notebook. "A ratio of three-to-one is best because it makes the horse chew his oats better."

"Yes, we took care of that, too," Lisa replied, a bit defensively.

Carole was caught up in her note taking. "Great, looks like you don't need me here, then. See you at TD's." She moved on. After all, she had a lot of other people to grade.

Carole found herself completely absorbed by her task. She was about to call it a day when she spotted May grooming Macaroni. Veronica was seated comfortably nearby, applying yet another new coat of red nail polish.

Tired though she was, Carole decided to help the

younger girl a little. After all, it wasn't May's fault she got stuck with Veronica.

Trying to appear casual, she approached. "Hi, May. Hi, Veronica."

"Hi, Carole," May called back. She flicked a dandy brush over the pony's rump, raising a small puff of dust.

Veronica glanced up and grunted before returning to her manicure.

Carole watched May's grooming technique. The girl was actually quite efficient and doing a decent job, but Carole's trained eyes noticed things an amateur might miss. "Hmmm, it looks like Mac's had some visitors."

May stopped what she was doing. "What do you mean?"

"Has anyone ever told you about botflys?"

"I don't think so. At least, not that I can remember."

Carole decided to be diplomatic. "Veronica, do you mind if I show May how to take care of bot eggs?"

This time Veronica didn't even bother to look up. "If it helps your conscience, who am I to stop you?"

That really made Carole steam, but she was determined not to let May and Macaroni suffer just because their Pony Partner was a jerk. She spent the rest of the afternoon teaching May about botfly eggs and how to use a block of wood wrapped in sandpaper to remove them from where they liked to attach themselves to horses. By the time she was finished she was past worrying about what Veronica and Betsy might have told the others. She could hardly wait to get to TD's and tell Lisa and Stevie about her amazing day.

4

STEVIE AND LISA were already tucked into their favorite booth at TD's when they spotted Carole coming through the door.

Stevie waved. "We were about to give up on you."

"Sorry. You wouldn't believe the day I've had." She sank into a seat. "I'm dying for a sundae. Have you ordered yet?"

"Not yet," said Stevie, flagging down the waitress. "We were waiting for you."

"Besides, Stevie couldn't make up her mind," Lisa added.

Stevie smiled and rubbed her hands together. "I have now," she said gleefully. "Watch the master at work."

When the waitress approached their table, she kept her eyes on Lisa and Carole, almost as if she were trying to avoid Stevie. Lisa ordered peppermint with hot fudge. Carole went with strawberry and whipped cream. "Hold the cherry, please."

All eyes turned to Stevie, whose creations were legendary. Lisa and Carole were of the opinion that she ordered the most revolting combinations so that nobody would ever ask for a taste. Still, they had to admit she had elevated it to an art form. Stevie cleared her throat. "I'd like a scoop of rum raisin and a scoop of bubble gum. I want marshmallow fluff on the raisin, and pineapple sauce on the gum." She put down the menu.

Looking relieved, the waitress turned to leave, but Stevie continued. "Of course, I'll be needing a few other toppings, as well." The woman stopped and sighed. Stevie paused for effect. "I'm thinking . . . whipped cream, Gummi Bears, and pistachios."

The waitress swallowed hard. "Will that be all?"

"Hmmm, have I forgotten anything?" Stevie looked at her friends, her eyes twinkling. "Oh yes, of course, silly me! Chocolate sprinkles, and cover it all with cherry juice but," she winked at Carole, "hold the cherry." Stevie saw the waitress's hand actually tremble as she wrote down the last of the order.

46

Lisa tried to suppress a fit of giggles. "You are going to drive that poor woman to a nervous breakdown."

Stevie was about to reply when she saw Alex coming through the door. "Uh-oh."

"What is it?" Carole asked, concerned.

"I forgot that I promised to meet my brothers at the mall."

"Still haven't figured out a present for your mom and dad?" Lisa asked sympathetically.

"Not even close," Stevie said, discouraged. "The more we talk about it, the more we fight. It's making me crazy."

"I'm sure you're not the only one," Carole said, noticing the look of annoyance on Alex's face.

"Stevie!" he snapped, stalking up to their table. "I've been waiting almost half an hour for you. Come on, the next bus is due any minute!"

"Hi, Alex," Lisa said.

Alex acknowledged their presence with a distracted wave but kept his eyes on his sister. "Will you move it? We're supposed to meet Chad and Michael at the pizza parlor."

Stevie rose to her feet reluctantly. "Sorry, guys, duty calls." She made a mock salute and started to leave.

"What about your sundae?" Lisa asked.

47

"Oh! I almost forgot." She turned to her brother. "Meet me at the bus stop. I'll be right out."

"You better, because I'm not gonna ask them to hold the bus for you."

As Alex left, Stevie hurried over to the waitress, who was now working behind the counter. "Excuse me, but have you started making my sundae yet?"

"No, I was saving that for last," she said glumly. "In case you changed your mind." She brightened suddenly. "Have you?"

"Not exactly. I'm afraid I have to cancel the order. Something came up."

The waitress visibly cheered up further, looking like a death row inmate who had gotten a last-minute pardon. "Oh, what a shame."

"Yeah, I know, but my friends will be staying."

"Well that's good, because I'm almost finished with theirs." She topped off some pink ice cream and juicy-looking red strawberries with a generous squirt of whipped cream.

Stevie suddenly had a brainstorm. She rushed over to the booth where Lisa and Carole were sitting.

"Aren't you supposed to be at the bus stop?" asked Carole, looking up.

"Yes, but I've got a great idea and I need you two to

help me carry it out." She took out a pen and grabbed a napkin. "I need you to order a pizza for me from Pizza Joe's in the mall."

"What do you want on it?"

Stevie looked back toward the ice cream counter and grinned, handing the pen and napkin to her friend. "Write this down."

When Stevie finished dictating the order she literally bolted for the door, leaving her two friends shaking their heads in wonder.

Carole studied the paper in her hand. "Her brothers are not going to believe this."

"I can hardly believe it myself," said Lisa.

Carole went off to make the call moments before the waitress arrived with their sundaes. "You know, your friend has quite a sense of humor."

Lisa knew she was referring to Stevie and not Carole. "Oh, you don't know the half of it," she said, looking toward the phones with a smile.

While Carole was placing Stevie's order, Lisa took a taste of frosty mint and chocolate and thought over the best way to express what she was feeling about the day's events.

"That's done," Carole said, slipping into the booth. "I'd love to see the look on her brothers' faces when that pizza arrives!" She snatched up her spoon and started on her sundae. "Yum. I think I really earned this today."

"You did work hard," Lisa said. "I think we were all doing our best."

"I'm sure of that, but you wouldn't believe some of the things I saw and heard going on at the stable!"

"It must be hard trying to keep up with so many riders," Lisa sympathized.

"Oh, believe me, it is."

"Maybe some of the mistakes you thought you saw or heard were because you arrived mid-lesson," Lisa suggested gently. "Maybe if you had heard the entire conversation . . ." She trailed off, unsure how to proceed.

Carole looked up from her sundae. "Are you worried about that thing with feeding Outlaw?"

Lisa was relieved. Perhaps this was going to be okay after all. "As a matter of fact, yes, I did want to talk to you about that."

"Don't worry about it, Lisa." Carole reached across the table and patted her hand. "I know you're still pretty new to riding, and I don't mind going the extra mile to make sure you keep Jasmine on the right track."

50

Lisa was dumbfounded. That wasn't what she had meant at all! Annoyed, she stabbed resentfully at her ice cream. Carole wasn't being fair. She had been doing fine with Jasmine, telling her everything she needed to know about feeding her pony properly. Just because Carole had come along in the middle of what they were doing was no reason for her to assume Lisa had forgotten some important detail. Carole had made her look bad in front of her Pony Partner, and now Lisa was concerned that Jasmine might lose confidence in her if it happened again.

"Look, Carole—" she began.

"Well, well, look who's here," a voice broke in. Turning, Lisa saw Veronica diAngelo and Betsy Cavanaugh approaching their table. "Tweedledum and Tweedledumber. The only one missing from this little tea party is the Mad Hatter."

The two girls slid into a seat right behind Lisa and Carole. "What are you going to order, Veronica?" Betsy asked in a loud voice. "The blue ribbon surprise?"

"No, Betsy," replied Veronica. "Unlike some people, I don't see a blue ribbon in my future—or yours either, for that matter."

51

Carole got to her feet and went over to the other girls' booth. "I might as well tell you right up front. You're absolutely right. You two will not be getting any blue ribbons from me."

Lisa was alarmed. How could Carole say something like that right out in the open? It made her look completely biased!

"On the other hand," Carole continued, "if you do a good job, your Pony Partners might!"

"Oh, Carole," Veronica smirked. "You don't have to say that simply because we're in public. Everyone at Pine Hollow knows where you stand."

"Veronica made sure of it," added Betsy, casually looking at her menu. "Just so none of those little kids would get their hopes up too high."

"Everybody is going to get a fair chance," Carole said, a little pleading creeping into her voice. "I mean that."

Veronica gave her a sly glance. "Don't worry about it, Carole, we know exactly what you *mean*." She winked at her friend. "Don't we, Betsy?"

Lisa could see that Carole was on the verge of tears. She desperately wished Stevie were there to handle Veronica, but she wasn't, so it was up to her. "Why Veronica," she said, peering over the back of her booth, "what a beautiful job you've done on your nail polish. I sure hope May Grover appreciated all the hard work you put into that today."

Much to Lisa's satisfaction, Veronica looked peeved. Lisa turned to her friend. "Carole, now that we're all clear on where we stand, don't you think we should finish up our sundaes and be on our way?"

"You're right," Carole said gratefully. "I still have a lot of work to do."

With that they sat down and determinedly ignored Veronica and Betsy for the rest of their snack.

STEVIE AND ALEX hustled from the bus stop to Pizza Joe's. When they got there they saw Michael and Chad standing by the doors at the front entrance, looking irritated. Stevie steeled herself. "I know, I know, don't say it," she said, hoping to cut off the inevitable recriminations before they began. "We're late."

"It's all her fault," Alex said accusingly.

"We could've grown old and died waiting on you," Chad growled, scowling at her.

Stevie was unable to resist. "Ah, I knew there was a reason I wasn't hurrying."

"I'm hungry," whined Michael.

"So what else is new?" asked Alex.

Chad put his arm around his little brother.

"Michael's right. If were gonna eat and still have time to look for a present for Mom and Dad, we've gotta get moving. It does actually take *time* to cook a pizza." He led the way inside.

"Don't worry about it, guys," Stevie said, bringing up the rear. "I have it all taken care of."

At those words her brothers stopped so abruptly that she ran right into Alex's back. All three of them turned to look at her. "Stevie, what have you done?" Alex said, squinting at her suspiciously.

She batted her eyes innocently. "Why, nothing terrible. Unless you call ordering ahead so that we wouldn't have to wait some kind of crime."

Her brothers all groaned with dismay.

"My treat," she added graciously.

The hostess returned to her post. "How many, please?"

"Four to sit down," Chad answered. "Probably one to eat." He glared at his sister.

As they were being seated, the woman offered menus.

"Oh, we won't be needing those," Stevie said, waving them away. "I called in an order."

"Your server will check on that for you." She left.

"Stevie, how could you do this?" demanded Chad.

54

"What?" Stevie asked with wide-eyed innocence.

"You ordered one of your bizarre combinations, didn't you?" he accused.

"Oh no!" wailed Michael. "I'm really, really hungry."

"Don't worry, Michael, you're gonna love this," she assured him.

Alex, elbows on the table and head in his hands, moaned. "What toppings did you put on it?"

"Stevie, this isn't funny," Chad reprimanded her. "It's one thing to play a practical joke, but the rest of us are actually hungry."

"Look," she said. "I simply preordered a pizza so that we could get on with looking for Mom and Dad's present. We *are* here to talk about Mom and Dad's anniversary gift, right?"

The boys all nodded.

"Then let's get on with it! Any suggestions?"

"How about some smelly bath soaps?" Michael offered.

"That's nice, Mike," agreed Alex. "But try to think bigger. How about a party? Like one of those *This Is Your Life* kind of things?"

"Not a bad idea," said Chad.

Stevie shook her head. "I don't think we have enough time left to get all their old friends together.

You know, like Dad's best man, Mom's maid of honor? What about a weekend at one of those exclusive spas?"

"Don't be stupid, Stevie," scoffed Chad. "Do you know how much those things cost?"

Stevie was annoyed by his superior attitude. "No, as a matter of fact, I don't. Do you?"

Chad had to admit he didn't. "But I bet it's a lot more than we have."

"Perfume?" suggested Michael.

"That's okay for Mom," Alex told him, clearly getting frustrated, "but we need something for the both of them! Get it?"

Stevie jumped to her younger brother's defense. "Don't snap at him. He's just trying to help."

"What about a barbecue?"

"We have barbecues all the time."

"Besides, that's not very romantic."

"I haven't heard you come up with anything brilliant."

"I'm doing my best!"

The discussion was quickly turning into a fight. Luckily, the waitress appeared, carrying a pizza tray. "This must be the Lake party," she said.

"That's us," Stevie said, relieved by the interruption. "How did you know?"

"Oh, the person who called in your order said to look for four young people having a big argument."

Stevie almost laughed aloud. Carole sometimes had a surprising sense of humor.

"One Stevie Lake special?" the server asked cheerfully.

"Oh great," muttered Alex. "Shall we leave you alone, Your Highness, so that you can eat your concoction in peace?"

"Let me guess," Chad said to the waitress. "Anchovies, pineapple, pepperoni, spinach, olives, onions, green pepper, and tuna fish."

"As a matter of fact, yes," she replied with a smile, "but you forgot the extra jalapeños."

Her three brothers glared at Stevie, who wouldn't meet their eyes.

"Of course, that's only one quarter of the pizza," continued the waitress. "The other three are all different. So, who gets the plain cheese?" She looked around the table expectantly.

"Plain cheese?" Michael echoed with wonder. "Me, me, me!"

"I should have known that. I've got a boy your age at home." She smiled as she served it. "Pepperoni and green pepper?"

"That's for him." Stevie pointed to her twin. "The

57

pepperoni, sausage, and mushrooms goes to my right." She gestured toward Chad. "And I think that leaves me with the works." Since her brothers appeared speechless, Stevie also handled who got which of the four different drinks.

"Let me know if you need any refills," the waitress said, moving away.

Michael took a sip of his drink. "Lemonade," he said delightedly. "Cheese pizza and lemonade. My favorite!"

"You ordered this before we even got here?" Alex asked, staring with wonder at his root beer.

"I thought it might get us all off on the right foot," Stevie answered.

Alex took a huge bite of his pizza. "Very cool, sis. Thanks."

Chad looked at his own meal, and then at Stevie. "You know, as a sister you're not always a *total* disaster."

"Thanks, Chad, same to you." She relished the rare moment of warmth with her siblings even more than her first bite of pizza. "Okay!" she said, talking with her mouth full. "Let's hit the stores after this. Things are going so well, maybe we'll get lucky and find something for Mom and Dad."

For once the Lake kids were in full agreement.

* * *

LISA AND CAROLE stayed only long enough at TD's to establish that they were not being driven out by Veronica and Betsy. Nevertheless, they were both relieved when they were outside again.

"You want me to walk you to the bus?" offered Lisa.

Carole started to say yes but suddenly realized she wasn't carrying her clipboard and judging papers. "Oh no!" she cried in dismay.

"What is it?" Lisa asked.

"My papers! I must have left them in my cubby, and it's not locked! I don't know how I could have been so careless."

"Don't worry about it. Nobody will bother them," said Lisa.

"I need to work on them tonight. I'll have to go back."

"Do you want me to go with you?" Lisa asked.

"No thanks. I can take care of it. See you tomorrow," said Carole.

She ran all the way back to Pine Hollow, arriving in the locker room anxious and out of breath. It was with great relief that she spotted her clipboard and folder on one of the benches, but as she reached out to retrieve them it suddenly occurred to her that they weren't where she had left them. She had put them in her cubby. With growing concern she quickly thumbed through the papers. Something was wrong. She was almost certain that someone had been going through them. *Why would someone do such a thing?* Carole wondered. An even better question was: *Who* would do such a thing?

STEVIE ARRIVED AT Pine Hollow on Sunday morning, running behind schedule as usual. She spotted Carole standing in the stable yard, clipboard in hand. Even though there was no official class scheduled, young riders were hustling here and there, trying to get in as much training time as possible. Stevie hurried over, attempting to retuck her shirt as she went. "Hi, Carole. Have you seen Corey around?"

"A little late, aren't you?" Carole said, scribbling something in her notebook.

Stevie felt a twinge of resentment as she watched Carole write. "A little," she admitted reluctantly, "but the good news is I think we've figured out a present for my parents."

Carole looked up. "Excellent. What did you decide on?"

Before she could answer, Stevie spotted Corey coming out of the stable, looking a little forlorn. "We'll talk later," she said, rushing off to help Corey before Carole could make any more notes.

Corey's face flooded with relief. "Stevie! I thought maybe I got the time wrong."

Stevie felt a little guilty. "No, it's my fault," she apologized. "How's Samurai coming?"

"I think he's ready to be saddled, but I wanted you to check to make sure I groomed him right first."

"Let's go look him over," Stevie said, cheerfully putting an arm around her charge. "Then I think we'll start with some ground work in the indoor ring."

It was almost an hour later before Stevie felt she could leave Corey to practice on her own. She spotted Lisa and Carole over by the outdoor ring and hurried to join them. "Good news, guys."

"I hear you've solved your problem," Lisa said. "What did you and your brothers decide on?"

"And how did you all ever manage to agree on *any-thing*?" Carole teased.

"I think the pizza did the trick," Stevie said, grinning.

"I'm sure they never saw that coming," laughed Lisa.

"Anyway, after we ate we were wandering around the mall when Michael started complaining about having to get dressed up for all the pictures Mom and Dad would want to take that day, and that did it!" Stevie snapped her fingers. "We're going to buy them a camera. A digital camera!"

"Oh, wow! I've seen those things demonstrated at the store," cooed Lisa. "They're amazing."

"The way your parents love to document every moment of your lives, I'm surprised they haven't bought one for themselves before now," Carole said, nodding approvingly. "Congratulations, Stevie. It really is the perfect present."

"I didn't realize you and your brothers had that kind of money saved up," Lisa said.

Stevie shrugged. "Apparently they're not that expensive."

Lisa looked surprised. "You don't think three hundred dollars is expensive?"

Stevie was puzzled. "Who said anything about three hundred dollars? Chad said it would be around eighty."

Carole put her hand on Stevie's shoulder. "I think he meant apiece. Eighty from each of you would come to around three hundred dollars."

Stevie went pale, then red. "Where does he think I'm going to get that kind of money? He may have that kind of cash, but Alex, Michael, and I sure don't!" she fumed.

"What are you going to do?" Lisa asked sympathetically.

"I'm going to the office to make a phone call," she answered grimly.

"Mrs. Reg won't let you use that phone, Stevie. It's only for emergencies."

"This *is* an emergency!" Stevie declared, striding away.

LISA'S EYES WERE drawn back to the ring, where Jasmine was working over four cavalletti set at their lowest level. The idea was for the rider to adjust the length of her horse's stride so that it would arrive three clear paces in front of the first pole. After that, the horse was to step, with one foot only, between each pole. The pair had negotiated the course fairly easily at a walk, but the posting trot was giving them trouble. Outlaw knocked one of the poles down with his back foot, then, turning to see what had happened behind him, he practically stepped on top of the next one. Not helping matters was the fact that Jasmine was completely off balance in the saddle and pulling too hard on the reins in an attempt to regain control of the situation.

"I'd better go talk to her," Lisa said, climbing through the fence.

"That sounds like a good idea," Carole agreed. Interested in hearing what kind of advice Lisa was going to give, she tagged along.

Jasmine was close to tears with frustration. "Lisa, it's hopeless. I can't make him do it."

Outlaw was also looking unhappy. Lisa put a soothing hand on his neck. "You're not adjusting his stride correctly before he reaches the three-out position. You two have to work together."

Carole was trying to be subtle about her eavesdropping, so she made herself useful by putting the cavalletti back up.

"I know," Jasmine said, obviously discouraged. "I can't make up my mind if he should be going slower or faster."

Lisa, who had already explained this several times, could feel her patience slipping. "Jasmine, I told you, it's not a matter of slower or faster, it's about the size of the step you're asking him to take." *I have to think of another way of describing what Jasmine needs to do, but how?* Her eyes fell on Carole. "Look, sit up straight, shoulders back, chin up, heels down. Good. Now get Outlaw collected, and I'll be right back."

Lisa hurried over to Carole and began helping to

reset the poles. "I can't seem to explain to Jasmine what she's doing wrong," she whispered urgently. "What can I say to her that will help?"

This was the moment Carole had dreaded. She was going to have to choose between being an impartial judge and being a supportive friend. She straightened up and looked Lisa square in the eyes. "I can't tell you that," she said firmly.

"What? Why not?" Lisa looked genuinely puzzled.

"Because it would be unfair to the other teams." Her friend's hurt expression made her feel terrible. Look, Lisa." She reached out to touch her shoulder. "This isn't like after the Horse Wise meeting. I'm not here to give advice. My job now is to see how you handle situations like this." She gestured toward Jasmine and Outlaw.

Lisa began to protest. "But Carole, you've always helped—"

Carole cut her off. "That was Carole your friend. Right now, I'm Carole the judge. We should both keep that in mind." Just then she spotted May at the far end of the ring. She and Macaroni were also working over cavalletti, and, as usual, Veronica was nowhere in sight. "I'm sorry, Lisa, I have to go."

Lisa watched Carole's retreating back with a mixture of hurt and anger. She was obviously going off to help

66

May—why wasn't that against her precious rules? Apparently now that she was a show judge, she didn't have time to help her old friends, only impress new ones.

Lisa returned to Jasmine and Outlaw, determined to solve this problem without Carole's help. That would show her.

"What did Carole say?" Jasmine asked.

Lisa thought quickly. "That she has every confidence in you and Outlaw mastering this technique."

"She does?" Jasmine said, obviously encouraged.

"Of course, and so do I." Lisa assured her. Even as she talked, her mind was racing furiously, trying to think of any training techniques from all the books she had read that might be useful in this situation. Then it came to her. "You know, Jasmine, Outlaw is looking a little frustrated," she said, patting his neck. "He was doing so well at the walk, I may have rushed it asking him to try it at the trot so soon. That's a lot to learn in one day."

Jasmine looked a little disappointed. "Do other ponies learn both in one lesson?"

Lisa tried to sound very casual. She wanted to take the pressure off both the pony and the rider. "Oh, there may be a few, but not many. Anyway, we're in no big rush. For Outlaw's sake, let's go back to cavalletti at the walk a few more times, then maybe I could saddle up Prancer and we could take a trail ride and talk about what we want to do in the next couple of weeks."

Jasmine brightened at the suggestion. "I think that's a good idea." The little girl smiled and patted her mount. "For Outlaw's sake."

Lisa smiled back.

STEVIE WAS FUMING. Mrs. Reg had reluctantly let her use the phone, but only for one short minute. She'd managed to get Chad on the line, but with Mrs. Reg nearby she'd been unable to bawl him out satisfactorily. He, on the other hand, with no one listening, had started yelling at her. As if this were her fault!

She had come out of the office looking for someone to air her grievances to when her eyes had fallen on Lisa and Carole. The two of them were in the outside ring, apparently deep in conversation. Carole was obviously passing on some great tip to help Lisa with her Pony Partner's schooling. Even as she had watched, Carole gave Lisa an encouraging pat on the shoulder before she left. Stevie felt a pang of jealousy. *Leave it to Lisa to appeal to Carole's soft heart*, she thought sullenly.

"Stevie?" Corey approached from behind. "I rode Samurai over the cavalletti at least ten times clean, then all of a sudden he started knocking them over. Can you come and tell me what I'm doing wrong?"

Stevie began to walk back to the indoor ring with her. "If he's already done it that many times right, then he's probably getting bored. Most likely we need to give him something harder or new to work on."

As the two of them passed by the gate to the outdoor ring, they met up with Lisa. "Have you got a minute, Stevie?" Lisa asked. "I need to talk to you about something."

Frustrated with her brothers and feeling resentful toward Lisa for taking advantage of Carole, Stevie failed to notice that her friend was genuinely upset. "Sorry, Lisa, can't do it right now," she said, breezing past her. "Why don't you ask Carole? I'm sure she'd be happy to help you out. Again." With that, she continued on her way.

CAROLE WORKED WITH May for fifteen minutes or so, during which she discovered that Veronica had gone for a trail ride. Instead of being resentful about it, as she had every right to be, May seemed quite pleased. Apparently Veronica had put things in such a way that the little girl actually believed being left alone to school herself was a vote of confidence. Carole bit her tongue, took notes, and offered encouragement where she could.

When she had finished with May, she continued her

rounds until she was satisfied she had visited every pair who had been working that morning. She had written down numerous observations in her book, intending to sort through them later.

Thinking of the notes reminded her about the evening before and her suspicion that someone had been going through her folder. If someone really had seen what she'd written, what good would it do them? Carole knew she couldn't change what had already happened, but she also knew she could take steps to make sure it would never happen again. From now until the judging was over, she would never leave the folder out of her sight.

6

STEVIE WALKED HOME in a bad mood. She couldn't remember the last time she had left Pine Hollow feeling this low. Usually life didn't get any better than spending a day in the company of friends and horses. Today, after winding up Corey's lesson, she had bolted for the door.

Irritably scuffing a stone from the path, she thought about Carole and Lisa. The two of them had been thick as thieves all day, and it seemed that Lisa had constantly been running to Carole for advice. Now that she thought about it, Stevie wasn't at all sure it was because Lisa had actually needed the advice. Maybe she was trying to score points with Carole. Of course, Carole would be loving the attention; she was

71

only human. No doubt Lisa would have some gold stars by her name that day in Carole's little notebook.

Stevie stopped, put her hands on her hips, and glared back the way she had come. That was another thing! She had worked really hard trying to get Corey ready for the show. They had made some good progress, but it seemed that every time something had gone wrong, she'd turned around to find Carole scribbling in that stupid book of hers. It just wasn't fair! The whole thing had irritated her so much that she'd decided she'd rather not have ice cream with Carole and Lisa as usual, so she'd slipped away without telling them she was leaving.

As she stumped along, her mind turned to a more urgent problem: her parents' anniversary present. With less than two weeks to the big day, she and her brothers were nowhere near to coming up with the perfect present. This morning she had bounded out of bed, relieved to know the problem had been solved; this afternoon they were right back where they had started. She wanted to scream!

"No, Jasmine, you're not pulling it tight enough!"

For the better part of an hour, Lisa had been patiently trying to teach the girl how to braid her pony's mane. "If you don't get the base tight, it's going to fall on the wrong side."

"But it's so hard," Jasmine complained for the umpteenth time. "Why can't we let it fall on the side it wants to?"

"I told you, it's traditional for the braids to be on the *off* side of the horse's neck, the opposite side you mount on, even if Outlaw's mane naturally flops to the other side." Lisa could understand Jasmine's frustration. Outlaw's thick, bushy mane wasn't making the job any easier. "Try using a little more setting gel and water," she suggested.

"Can't we start with his tail?" Jasmine asked hopefully. "That doesn't have to fall in any direction but down, right?"

"There's no point in learning how to do the tail if you can't do the mane," Lisa said.

"Why not?" Jasmine asked as she continued to struggle with a braid.

"Because you can ride Outlaw in a show with just his mane braided, or you can ride him with his mane and tail braided, but you can't show your horse with only the tail braided."

"Why not?" Jasmine demanded again.

"It's tradition!" Lisa snapped. She looked despairingly at the messy tangle of braids decorating Outlaw's neck. He bore more of a resemblance to Medusa than to a show pony. The idea of giving up on this particular aspect of Jasmine's training tempted Lisa. It certainly wasn't required. However, a braided mane and tail were the final touch to a formal turnout for a hunter, and she was determined that her charges were going to look their absolute best at the Horse Wise rally. Even if it killed all three of them!

CAROLE PULLED THE heavy black curtain more tightly around her and stared out through a tiny opening in the folds at the locker area, waiting for someone to take the bait. The more she had thought about someone invading her private things, the more it had made her angry. The angrier she got, the less she had been able to think about anything else. It had even interfered with her judging duties, because every time she walked up to a student, part of her mind wondered, *Are you the one?*

Realizing she wasn't going to be able to concentrate until she solved this mystery, she had resolved to set a trap. Late in the afternoon, while many of the riders were winding down their lessons, she went around to say her good-byes. As she did she made sure to mention that she was leaving and that she was so tired she would forget her head if it wasn't attached. It was her hope that the person who had looked at her notes last time might try it again. Leaving the notebook on the bench in plain sight, she had hidden herself behind the curtain and was waiting to catch them red-handed.

Unfortunately, that had been some time ago, and the few riders who had come and gone had all failed to even notice the bait, let alone take it. She was almost ready to give up when she heard someone else enter the locker room. Holding her breath, she tried to be as quiet as possible, ready to jump out and confront the cheater. Within moments, however, it became apparent that whoever it was had gotten what they were looking for and left. Her judging folder remained undisturbed where she had left it, out in plain, tempting sight.

With a sigh, Carole decided to call it quits for the night. She collected her folder and switched off the light, refusing to be discouraged. Sooner or later the culprit would make a mistake, and when they did she would be there to catch them!

AT FIRST STEVIE had intended to head straight home, but it dawned on her that as soon as she arrived she would have to confront her brothers, and she didn't feel up to that. Instead she let her feet carry her in any old direction. After a while she looked up and was startled to find herself standing practically in front of TD's.

It must have been force of habit, she thought. Worried that Lisa and Carole would show up at any minute, she was preparing to beat a hasty retreat when she spotted Veronica diAngelo coming out of the shop, licking delicately at an ice cream cone. An idea occurred to her. Normally she had no use for the snotty girl, but today might be different. There wasn't much that Veronica could do right, but even Stevie had to admit that she had a talent for one thing: shopping.

"Hi, Veronica," Stevie greeted her in the friendliest voice she could muster. "What a great piece of luck. You're just the person I've been looking for."

"That's more than I can say about you," Veronica replied, looking at her suspiciously. "What do you want?"

"Actually, I could use some advice," Stevie admitted reluctantly.

"Cut your hair, tuck in your shirt, and drop those two losers you hang with," Veronica said.

Under normal circumstances that would have been the end of any civil conversation between the two of them, but Stevie was desperate. "Ha, ha. Good one." She forced herself to chuckle. "I'm serious, though."

"Not dressed like that you're not," Veronica snorted.

Stevie bit her lip with annoyance. "My brothers and I need to get an anniversary present for our parents, and I thought you might have some ideas. Can I ask what you got your mom and dad for their last anniversary?"

"You can ask," Veronica replied.

"Oh come on, it's not like it's a state secret or something," Stevie coaxed.

"If you must know, I bought them a digital camera."

Stevie almost groaned out loud.

A white Mercedes drove into the parking lot and pulled up to the curb next to them. Veronica waited for the chauffeur to get out and open the door for her. "Chilton, you're late, I actually had to wait! And I had to talk to *her*," she complained, nodding toward Stevie. She slid inside and the driver shut the door. The smoked glass window descended noiselessly. "You know, Lake, if I were your parents, the thing I'd love most about you would be your absence. Why don't you and your brothers run away with the circus? I'm sure that would make them happy."

Before Stevie could think of an answer, the window slid closed and the car pulled away.

If she had been in a bad mood before, it was nothing compared to the one she was in now. Betrayed by her friends, hindered by her brothers, and now bested by Veronica diAngelo! She had the sudden urge to go home and hide in bed for the rest of the day.

When she reached her house, the level of noise that greeted her was earsplitting. Her brothers were in the middle of a huge argument.

"You are so stupid I can't even believe it!" Alex screamed at Chad.

"This from the moron who wants me to get him tickets to a Death Drop concert?" Chad spat back.

"At least *I'm* trying to use my head."

"For what? A doorstop?"

Stevie dropped her things and tried to get between them. "You guys, cut it out!"

Chad pushed her aside. "Butt out, Stevie! He's been asking for this all day!"

"Me?" yelled Alex, clearly outraged. He turned to Stevie. "Ever since you called here this morning he's been a total jerk. He even made Michael cry!"

"Well, if Stevie hadn't bitten my head off over the camera thing . . . ," Chad responded heatedly.

Stevie couldn't believe her ears. Somehow it was all her fault? "Hey, wait a minute. If you hadn't suggested the camera, we might have thought of something else by now!"

"Oh great, blame it all on me!" Chad bellowed at the top of his lungs.

"I do!" shouted Alex.

Stevie stepped back and put her hands over her ears. She couldn't take much more of this. "Shut up!" she hollered over the bedlam. "Will you two shut up for one second! Mom and Dad will be home any minute and we can't let them see us like this."

Her words seemed to reach the two boys, because they fell into an angry silence and settled for merely glaring at each other instead. Stevie seized the moment to beat a retreat, grabbing her stuff and heading to her room. "You know," she yelled at them from her doorway, "Veronica diAngelo was right. Things would be a lot better around here if you guys would run away and leave the rest of us in peace!" She slammed the door with all her might.

The tears started even before she could reach her bed. She flung herself down and muffled her sobs in her pillow, kicking her feet and pounding her mattress in rage.

Eventually, after the worst of it was over, she reached for her stuffed blue dog, Wubbie, burying her tearstained cheeks in its soft fur. As she reached for a tissue to blow her nose, her eyes fell on the telephone.

Almost every time in Stevie's life when she was badly upset, her Saddle Club friends somehow sensed it and came to her rescue. She watched the phone expectantly. Nothing happened. She looked at Wubbie. "Should I?" she asked him. His soulful face was sympathetic but noncommittal. Stevie reached for the phone.

She tried Carole's house first. She was disappointed when she got no answer but a little relieved that Colonel Hanson hadn't picked up, either. Stevie loved Carole's dad, and they both shared a passion for bad jokes, but today she wasn't feeling very funny. Next she tried Lisa's house. Again there was no answer. She put down the phone and leaned back against her pillow. She could picture her two friends down at TD's, laughing and chatting. *They didn't even invite me*, she thought resentfully, conveniently forgetting that she had snuck out of Pine Hollow in order to avoid just that.

Feeling very sorry for herself, she rolled over on her side and snuggled Wubbie even closer.

WEDNESDAY AFTERNOON, STEVIE found herself in the unusual circumstance of walking home from the bus stop with her brothers. Since the big blowup on Sunday, the four of them had managed to reach a truce, and now they were all racking their brains over the elusive anniversary present idea.

For her part Stevie was glad she had a problem to focus on: It took her mind off the previous day's riding class. Tuesday sessions were for the more advanced riders, so the under-twelve Pony Partners had been absent, but they hadn't been the only thing missing that day. Gone also was The Saddle Club camaraderie. It seemed to her that she, Lisa, and Carole had all gone out of their way to avoid being together. Every time she *had* made an effort to chat with them, they had both made it clear they weren't interested. Carole had been completely distracted, and Lisa was cool and distant, barely making eye contact. That had hurt. Now she forced herself to focus on the problem at hand. "Alex, remember in the pizza parlor you mentioned a *This Is Your Life* kind of party?"

"Yeah, you shot it down," he replied. "And you were right. We wouldn't have had time to get it together."

"Maybe I was only half right," Stevie said thoughtfully.

"You've got something in mind?" Chad asked.

Stevie stopped walking. "Why are we making this so complicated? Let's throw them a great surprise party with all their best friends from here in town."

Her brothers looked at her. Stevie was afraid they were all about to start making fun of her, but instead, they actually began smiling.

"You know, you're absolutely right," Chad said. "Maybe we've been blowing this 'present' thing all out of proportion."

"Yeah," agreed Alex. "Maybe the best gift of all would be to have people they like, and who like them, come over and talk. Adults like to talk."

"And eat," added Michael.

"You know, if we're going to do this, we're going to

82

have to do it right." Stevie looked at each of her brothers. "*Are* we going to do this?"

Everyone smiled. They were all in agreement!

"Okay, we've only got ten days; we need to get organized!" Stevie said, beginning to walk again. "First of all we'll need a place to hold it. I can think of a couple of places right off the bat, so maybe I should be in charge of that."

"Great, you got it," said Chad. "By the way, I think Michael had a good point. We're definitely going to need some eats."

"Not just chips and dips, though. We should get fancier stuff," Michael added.

"Hey! I know this guy in school whose brother is dating this really cool girl," Chad said thoughtfully.

"Alert the media," Alex teased.

Chad shot him a look. "It so happens her father works for a catering business. Maybe she could help us get a deal."

"Excellent, Chad," said Stevie. "You're in charge of the food. What else will we need?"

"How about some music?" Chad asked. "We should get a live band. It's much classier than CDs."

"I know a guy who's in a band," Alex said. "I could check and see if they can play that night. I bet they wouldn't charge us much."

"What about me?" asked Michael. "What can I do?"

Stevie considered for a moment. "How about the decorations? I think you'd be really good at that."

Michael beamed at the suggestion. "Oh yeah! I want to do the decorating. I can already think of lots of things to do."

"All right then, we've finally got a plan!" enthused Stevie. "Now, we've got a lot to do." Suddenly she felt a little pang of sadness. Normally she would have relied heavily on Lisa to help get things organized, and Carole was always wonderful at taking care of the little details. It looked like this time she was going to have to rely on herself and her brothers.

As soon as they got home, Michael headed straight to his room to make a list of things he'd need for decorating, Alex ran off to ask his friend about the band, Chad grabbed the kids' phone to call about catering, and Stevie got on her parents' line to the country club.

Unfortunately it only took a few minutes for her to find out that they would only rent rooms to current members. Disappointed but not discouraged, she moved on to plan B, and she quickly dialed the number of her dad's service club. He was a member in good standing, so they couldn't possibly turn her down. It turned out they were willing to rent her a room, but she hadn't called far enough in advance and they were all booked up. Out of curiosity Stevie asked how much it would have cost, then nearly fell out of her chair at the answer. She hung up the phone with a panicky feeling in her chest. Renting a hall for the party was going to cost more than a digital camera!

Stevie went to find Chad, hoping he might be able to think of an alternative. She found him in the living room with a shocked look on his face.

"Do you have any idea how much it costs to feed fifty people?" he asked in a shaky voice.

"More than a digital camera?" Stevie guessed.

Chad nodded. "No wonder Mom and Dad keep complaining about the grocery bill."

Alex swung through the front door, a grin on his face. "I got the band, and they only want twenty-five dollars!" he said excitedly.

That sounded too good to be true. "What's the catch?" Stevie asked suspiciously.

"Turns out they only know three songs," he said sheepishly. "But it's no big deal."

Chad looked skeptical. "How do you figure that?"

Alex flopped on the couch. "Mom and Dad are always complaining that our music all sounds the same, right? So they'll never notice it's the same three songs over and over!"

Stevie sank into a chair. Their ship of dreams had definitely sprung some leaks.

CAROLE WANDERED RESTLESSLY around the nearly deserted stable. She had come by to set her trap again, but to her disappointment none of the Pony Partner teams were around, so hiding behind the changing curtain would be a waste of time. Time she didn't really have to waste. She knew she should have been working on organizing her judging papers, but she was finding herself more and more reluctant to do so. It wasn't this unsolved mystery that was distracting her, either. She was lonely. She tossed her judging folder none too gently onto a bench, sending some of the loose papers fluttering to the floor. She glared at it resentfully.

At first she had been delighted to have been chosen for this job, but now all she wanted was to get back to normal. The responsibility was weighing heavily on her, especially since she had to carry it alone. Any other time Lisa and Stevie would have been right by her side, cheering her on and helping her nab the culprit. No doubt Stevie would have come up with a much better plan than hiding behind a dumb curtain, and Lisa would have put her razor-sharp mind to the problem and figured out who had done it by a logical process of elimination. It didn't seem fair that she couldn't ask them for help, that she had to keep her distance from them until this whole business was over.

"I thought I heard someone in here." Mrs. Reg, Max's mother and Pine Hollow's stable manager, stood larger than life in the doorway. "Working on the show, I see." She eyed the mess on the bench and floor.

Embarrassed to have been caught in what was basically a tantrum, Carole hurried to collect the papers. "Oh, hi, Mrs. Reg. Yes, I was sorting through some things."

"That's quite a load of papers you have there. It's a big responsibility Max has handed you. You must be very proud."

"I guess," Carole said, trying to drum up some enthusiasm.

"I remember a long time ago Max's father had a pony named Cobweb," Mrs. Reg said, leaning against the doorjamb. "We named him that because he was a beautiful silvery gray color, and his mane and tail were so soft. More like human hair than pony hair. Know what I mean?"

"Yes, of course," Carole acknowledged. She knew what was coming: Mrs. Reg was going off on one of her stories. She did that from time to time. You could rarely tell what had set her off or what any of it had to do with you, but once she had begun the best thing was to let her carry on until she was finished.

"He was a lovely pony, that one. He took to his saddle training like a duck to water, and gentle . . . Well, he was a big favorite with the young riders, as you can imagine. The parents loved him, too, because they knew they could always rely on him to take care of their kids. Sometimes it seemed like that pony was doing more of the teaching than my Max was." She chuckled.

Carole smiled politely, wondering where this story was going.

"One day Max got it into his head that he wanted to use Cobweb for driving. I guess he thought he would make a very pretty sight pulling a little cart." Mrs. Reg's eyes had a faraway look. "Cobweb, on the other hand, had other thoughts on the matter. He made it very clear that he wanted nothing to do with the whole thing. In fact, when he saw anyone coming at him with that tack, he'd snort and paw and lay his ears back so hard it looked like he didn't have any."

Carole laughed at the idea of such a beautiful, gentle pony trying to act so fierce. Kind of like an angry kitten.

"When it came to his training, Cobweb was slow to

learn, but Max knew it wasn't because he was stupid, it was that he simply didn't enjoy that part of being a pony. Of course, if you had known my husband at all, you'd know that if he thought something was for the best, he couldn't be deterred."

Mrs. Reg seemed to have come to the end of the story as abruptly as she had started it. While this didn't surprise Carole, she couldn't resist asking one question. "So did Cobweb become a great driving pony in spite of how he felt at the beginning?"

"Oh no, dear. He was pretty good at it, but you could tell he never really enjoyed it. Still, he learned what he needed to know." She looked at her watch. "Oh my, I really must go."

Mrs. Reg was on her way back to her office before Carole could even say good-bye. As usual she had no idea what to make of the story or why Mrs. Reg had told it to her.

Since it was fairly obvious she wasn't going to accomplish anything by hanging around the stable, Carole headed out for the bus stop. Maybe tomorrow something would shake loose.

FRIDAY AFTER SCHOOL, Lisa was hard at work with Jasmine. She took out a pencil and book and presented them to the girl.

Jasmine examined the book curiously. It was dark blue with a white unicorn on the front, and inside were lined white pages, waiting to be filled. "It's so pretty!" she exclaimed, running her hand over the cover. "But what's it for?"

Lisa sat on a bale of hay and patted the space next to her. "One of your jobs as Outlaw's rider is to keep track of his records. Visits to the vet, when he had his shoes fixed last, how much he eats, that kind of thing," she explained. "You could jot it down on any old piece of paper, but I thought you might like something a little more special."

Jasmine's eyes were shining. "Oh, thank you! I'll take real good care of it."

"I know you will," Lisa said, smiling at the girl's enthusiasm. "Now," she said, reaching into her shirt pocket and extracting a folded piece of paper, which she handed to Jasmine, "even though the show skills rally will take place here at Pine Hollow, we want to treat it like the under-twelve show. I want you to make a checklist. On one side write down all the things you think Outlaw may need to have with him for the show, and on the other side write down everything you're going to need yourself that day."

Jasmine promptly began to scribble. "This is going to be easy."

Lisa said nothing. She knew it sounded simple enough, but in the excitement of competition, young riders frequently forgot important items. By having Jasmine make this list early, Lisa intended to make sure that no essential piece of equipment would be overlooked on show day.

"Hi, Jasmine. Hi, Lisa," called Corey, skipping across the stable yard toward them.

Lisa was surprised to see her. She hadn't anticipated

that Corey and Stevie might want to put in some work that day as well.

Jasmine looked up from her paper. "Hi, Corey. You still want to meet for a soda after class?"

"Of course, and let's ask May, too." Corey turned to Lisa. "Do you know where Stevie is?"

"Have you tried inside?" Lisa asked.

"Not yet. I thought you might have come together, you being best friends and all."

Her words made Lisa cringe. Not only had she not seen Stevie or Carole since Tuesday's lesson, she hadn't even spoken to them on the phone. For the members of The Saddle Club, that was unprecedented. She made up her mind to do something about it. "Come on, Corey, I'll walk in with you," she offered, jumping up from the hay bale. "Jasmine, keep working, I'll check your list when I get back."

Stevie, who was waiting for Corey by Samurai's stall, looked surprised to see Lisa.

"Hi, Stevie, how's it going?" Lisa asked, trying to sound casual and not wanting to make a big deal about their recent lack of communication.

"Uh, hi. Things are great," Stevie answered. "You working with Jasmine today?"

"Yeah. You working with Corey?"

"Yeah."

There was an awkward silence. Corey was looking at the two of them curiously. "Corey," Stevie said, "start cleaning Samurai, but don't tack him up; we're not going to be riding today."

The girl hurried into the stall, obviously eager to get started.

Lisa decided to make the first gesture. "I'm sorry I haven't called you. School stuff kept me really busy." It wasn't quite true, but she wasn't ready to talk about the real reasons yet.

"I know what you mean. I haven't had a second to myself!" Stevie responded with sincere exasperation. "In fact, I haven't talked to Carole, either."

One part of Lisa was relieved to hear it. Ever since she had asked Carole for help and had been refused, she had felt out of sync with her friends and had been afraid that Stevie and Carole might be talking behind her back. But another, larger, part of her was alarmed. *None* of The Saddle Club had been speaking to each other. Something had to be done immediately. "I was thinking," she said. "We haven't been able to get together all week, so what about a sleepover? I could ask Max if we could use the hayloft tomorrow night."

Stevie hesitated, a slight frown clouding her face. Lisa was surprised and a bit hurt that Stevie wasn't jumping at her suggestion. "Look, if you don't want to—"

"No, no, of course I want to," Stevie said.

Lisa was still puzzled by her initial hesitation. Was it possible Stevie didn't want to spend time with her because they were in competition with each other? Stevie could be very competitive, but perhaps there was more to it. The important thing was to get them all together so that they could clear the air and get back to normal. "One of us should ask Carole. Have you seen her around?"

"No, but then Corey and I haven't made any *mistakes* today."

Lisa was taken aback by the resentment in Stevie's voice. Perhaps Stevie and Carole were having problems of their own. "It wouldn't be a Saddle Club meeting without her, though. Right?"

Stevie looked ashamed. "Of course not. Tell you what, we'll call her later when we finish our lessons."

"Great. I'll go clear it with Max."

"Good. Meantime, I've got to get to work with Corey. I'm going to teach her about braiding today. Wish us luck."

"Believe me, I do!" said Lisa, recalling her own exasperating experience trying to teach Jasmine that particular skill. She hurried off to find Max, who, as it turned out, was in the hayloft and didn't mind at all if they made use of it Saturday night.

It was with a much lighter heart that Lisa returned to her work with Jasmine. She carefully checked the girl's list. "Are you sure there's nothing else you can think of?"

Jasmine shook her head.

"Okay, let's go to the tack room. You're going to get Outlaw ready for a show using only the items that you put on this list, and if you've forgotten something . . ." She shrugged, leaving the sentence unfinished.

On their way to the tack room they passed by Samurai's stall. Lisa couldn't resist peeking in to see how it was going. Samurai's mane was a neatly braided work of art.

"Excellent work, Corey," Stevie was saying.

Corey grinned at her Pony Partner. "It always looked so hard when I watched my dad do it, but you made it seem easy."

Lisa bit her lip. In some areas Stevie was obviously a much better teacher than she was. Slightly depressed again, she followed Jasmine to the tack room and watched as the younger girl collected the items on her list. As she supervised, she mulled the braiding problem over in her head. It would really benefit Jasmine to have Stevie teach her how to braid, but it wouldn't be fair of Lisa to ask unless she could offer Stevie something in return. The question was, what?

"That's everything on the list," Jasmine announced.

Lisa eyed the pile on the ground. "Okay, then that's all you've got to work with. If you've forgotten something, you'll have to do without it, and so will Outlaw."

Actually Lisa had already spotted a couple of items missing from the list. It would be interesting to see how Jasmine was going to clean her pony's feet without a hoof pick or get him water without a bucket. This exercise would certainly help her learn some organizational skills. Which gave Lisa an idea. Stevie might be really good at teaching braiding, but she was notoriously bad at record keeping and organization, an area Lisa excelled in. Maybe she had something to offer in exchange after all! She hurried off to find Stevie and ask her.

COREY HAD DONE such a good job on Samurai's mane that Stevie decided they could move on to his tail. "We always use a French braid on a hunter's tail," she explained, "but there are two different ways to do it. The first one I'm going to teach you is the under braid, which is the easiest. Once you can do that, we'll move on to the over method."

"That makes sense," said a voice from outside the stall.

Stevie turned, startled to see Carole. For some reason, in spite of the fact that Carole had sounded approving, Stevie felt like she had been caught doing something wrong. She resented the feeling. "Carole, I didn't expect to see you here today."

Lisa came hurrying down the hall. "Carole, what are you doing here?"

"I decided I needed a good old-fashioned trail ride, and I was hoping you two might want to come along."

"I'm sorry, but I really can't," Stevie said. "I still have a lot of work to do with Corey."

"Me too," said Lisa. "Only with Jasmine, of course," she added.

Stevie felt bad when she saw Carole's disappointment. "Lisa did have a great idea, though. She suggested a hayloft sleepover tomorrow night. That is, if Max approves."

"He already did," Lisa told them happily. "So what do you think, Carole, you up for a long overdue Saddle Club meeting tomorrow?"

"Tomorrow night?" Carole said. "Well . . . I'll have to check with Dad. I think there might be one of those all-night old-movie marathons on, and you know how he loves to have me watch with him. But if not, I guess I can. I think." She strode off down the hall.

Stevie exchanged glances with Lisa, who seemed equally surprised by Carole's unenthusiastic response. Of course they all had to check with their parents first, but that was hardly ever a problem. They all automatically assumed they could do these things until they were told differently. This time Carole seemed to assume right off the bat that she *wouldn't* be able to.

Lisa put her hands on her hips. "What's up with her these days?"

Stevie shook her head. "I have no idea. It's not like she's the one under pressure to perform."

"Yeah," agreed Lisa. "She's the ringmaster and we're the performing ponies. Speaking of which, I've got to get back to Jasmine."

Stevie spent the rest of the afternoon perfecting Corey's tail braiding technique and reminding the girl not to get so absorbed by her work that she placed herself in a position to be kicked. From time to time she noticed Carole hanging around the locker room, which struck her as odd since she had said she was going on a trail ride. Perhaps Carole had changed her mind when she found out Stevie and Lisa couldn't go with her. Stevie considered talking to her about it, but she needed to wrap things up and get home quickly. Her aunt was going to be visiting them for a few days and the last thing Stevie wanted was to upset her parents by being late for dinner. She was even determined to be nice to her brothers for the entire meal!

LISA AND HER Pony Partner were finishing up when Corey stopped by the stall to see if Jasmine was ready to leave. During the course of the afternoon, Jasmine had discovered several items she needed that had been missing from her list. Now, after making the additions, she and Lisa were both secure in the knowledge that come show day they would have everything they needed at their fingertips.

"Why don't you go ahead?" Lisa said to Jasmine.

"But I haven't put all the equipment away yet."

"I can take care of it this time," Lisa offered. "You did a good job on that list. You can call it a day."

Jasmine smiled at her gratefully. "Thanks, Lisa, you're the best."

Lisa watched the duo hurry away, then picked up the grooming kit and a few other scattered items, returned them to their proper places, and took one final look around to make sure all was as it should be. As she headed for the locker room, she remembered she had forgotten to ask Stevie about the braiding lesson. Oh well, she could ask her tomorrow at the sleepover.

The room was quiet as she entered. Not bothering to turn on the lights, since there was still enough daylight for her to see by, she quickly scooped up her things and headed for the door. As she was about to exit, she stopped short and turned back. Carole's cubby was open. Worse, her judging folder was sticking out where anybody could get to it! Lisa remembered the ice cream parlor and how worried her friend had been that something might happen to the folder. Without another thought, Lisa moved quickly to the locker. She was reaching out to shove the items safely back inside when Carole ripped open the changing curtain, shouting, "Got ya!"

Lisa was so startled she actually gave a small scream.

Carole stared, her face a mask of astonishment and anger. "You? You're the one who did it?"

"Carole, you scared me half to death!" cried Lisa, annoyed by what she thought was her friend's childish prank to frighten her.

"All this time I've been racking my brains trying to figure out who had gotten into my folder, but it never once occurred to me it might have been Stevie or you!" Carole's voice was shaking and her eyes were full of tears. "I thought I knew you, but I don't know you at all!" With that she ran out of the room, clutching her folder to her chest.

Lisa was in a state of bewilderment. *What just happened here?* Carefully she replayed the scene in her mind: reaching for Carole's folder, then Carole jumping out from behind the curtain where she had been hiding. Had it been a trap? Did Carole believe someone had been cheating and reading her notes? And did she really believe that that someone was *her*? Lisa was almost in tears at the idea. How could Carole think that? They were supposed to be best friends! Friends trusted each other. Friends helped each other. Maybe they weren't friends after all.

As Lisa headed for home, the tears rolled freely down her cheeks. What was happening to The Saddle Club?

9

SATURDAY ALL THE riders gathered at Pine Hollow. They started the day with an unmounted meeting, where Max and Carole showed them how to prepare a horse for traveling in a trailer and the easiest way to load an animal, then everyone moved to the tack room for a lesson on how to clean and maintain their equipment.

Distractedly, Carole added a capful of ammonia to the water bucket to help cut grease and remove dirt from the leather. Her mind kept wandering back to the other evening when she had caught Lisa trying to sneak a peek at her judging folder. She couldn't get over the betrayal. It made her both angry and heartbroken. Lisa was the last person on the planet she would ever have suspected of snooping.

Max signaled Carole that he was ready to start. "You begin by using a moist, not wet, sponge, to take off the surface dirt," he said, wiping at the seat of a saddle. "When the tack is clean but still damp, rub glycerin saddle soap into it. If you work up a lather you're using too much, which can dull the shine and eventually crack the leather."

Carole's eye happened on Stevie, who was sitting at the back with Corey, well away from Lisa and Jasmine. Again, she felt a twinge of annoyance and disappointment. Stevie seemed totally preoccupied these days with her parents' upcoming anniversary. Carole couldn't help feeling that Corey was getting the short end of the stick. From what she had observed, Stevie was neglecting good record keeping—Corey's equipment box was complete chaos, and Carole was fairly certain they hadn't yet gotten around to setting a date to have Samurai's shoes checked before the show.

"Carole. Carole?" Max looked at her expectantly. "May I have the cloth, please?"

With a guilty smile, she handed it to him. She should have been paying better attention.

"You don't rinse the soap off," Max continued. "Instead, use a soft cloth to buff the leather to raise the shine."

Carole noticed May was riveted on everything Max said and did. Veronica, on the other hand, was sitting in a corner at the back of the room, reading a book. *Well that's no great surprise. At least Veronica makes no attempt to conceal her real nature*, she thought.

Max was winding up the demonstration. "To make the leather even more supple, you can use a nonoily leather dressing, but never, never use neat's-foot oil. It will only make things dark and greasy."

LISA STIRRED RESTLESSLY in her seat. For the first time in a long time she was actually wishing she was any place but Pine Hollow. That terrible scene with Carole kept replaying over and over in her head, making it impossible for her to focus on what Max was saying. Why would Carole assume she had been trying to cheat? Didn't she know her better than that? After all the things they'd been through, Carole should at least have given her the benefit of the doubt.

Jasmine interrupted her thoughts. "That was really useful, wasn't it, Lisa? I'm going to make sure Outlaw's tack is sparkling on the day of the show. He's going to be the best-turned-out pony in the arena!"

Lisa smiled on the outside, but on the inside she was

grimacing. Unless Jasmine could learn to master the art of braiding, poor Outlaw was going to be one of the frumpiest contestants in the ring that day. Lisa hadn't had a chance to talk to Stevie about swapping Pony Partner favors yet. She had intended to talk to her at the sleepover, but now she wasn't sure she even wanted to have one. Carole had already told Stevie that she wasn't going to be able to make it, which, of course, had come as no surprise to Lisa.

"Okay," Max said. "Time to get your horses and ponies ready for the mounted portion of today's lesson, and don't be late."

Lisa hurried to Prancer's stall, where she tacked up as quickly as she could. She wanted a few extra minutes to look over Jasmine's work on Outlaw before class started.

When she saw her Pony Partner, she was delighted. "Good job, Jasmine. Outlaw looks very nice. Let's take the horses outside."

As they came out of the stable, Lisa blinked at the bright sunshine. Although it was a lovely spring day, she couldn't really enjoy it because she was so depressed by Carole's accusation. At least the horses seemed to like it. They snorted and sucked in large gulps of fresh air. Outlaw took a playful nip at a piece of straw that went dancing by.

Suddenly Carole's voice broke the calm. "Jasmine!" she said sternly. "You never, ever let your horse eat while he's wearing his bit. Especially when he's getting ready to enter the ring."

Jasmine looked surprised at the harsh tone of Carole's voice. "I wasn't—He—" she stammered.

"It's not your fault, Jasmine," Carole said in a gentler tone. "Someone should have taught you better, that's all." She moved on without even glancing Lisa's way.

Lisa was both furious and humiliated. How could Carole have done something like that? Jasmine hadn't been letting her pony eat, he had just been playing around with a wisp of hay!

OUTSIDE THE RING Stevie and Corey sat in companionable silence, waiting for Max to announce the start of class. Their mounts had snuffled each other's noses by way of greeting and now stood quietly side by side. From the corner of her eye, Stevie caught sight of Carole approaching, clipboard in hand. Her heart began to sink. "Hi, Carole," Stevie said in what she hoped was a cheerful voice. "Not riding today?"

Carole strolled up to Samurai and placed a hand on his haunch. "Not today, Stevie. Some of us have to put business before pleasure," she said pointedly. "Got to go." She gave Samurai a pat on his flank and a puff of dust rose into the air. A frown crossed her face. "Looks like you were in a hurry grooming Samurai today, Corey."

"Not at first," Corey said, defending herself. "I just had a hard time finding his dandy brush, and by the time I did, I had to hurry." She looked at the ground, obviously embarrassed by this admission.

Carole started scribbling on her notepad. "I saw what your grooming kit looked like this morning, Corey, and I have to say I'm surprised that you and Samurai made it out of the stable at all." She looked directly at Stevie. "Maybe you two need to get a bit more organized."

Stevie found herself glaring at Carole's back as she moved off toward May and Macaroni. What Carole had done was plain mean. So Samurai wasn't at his absolute best today, so what? It wasn't like this was a show day! So her Pony Partner wasn't the most organized one in the group. But Corey had lots of other strengths. Strengths that Carole seemed to be going out of her way to ignore or belittle. Carole had changed so much lately that Stevie could only think that she had let this whole judging thing go to her head. She sighed sadly. Too bad Carole wasn't going to come to the sleepover with her and Lisa. Maybe between the two of them they could have brought her back to her senses.

It didn't help matters any when, a few minutes later, they overheard Carole praising May and her pony in the most glowing of terms.

After class, Stevie found Lisa cleaning Prancer's stall.

"Stevie, would you mind very much if we postponed the sleepover?" Lisa asked.

"Is something wrong?"

"Um, well, you know Carole can't make it," Lisa said hesitantly. "It really couldn't be a Saddle Club meeting without her."

"You're right. We should do it when we can all be there." *Besides,* Stevie thought, *I could use the time to work on the anniversary party.*

"We'll do it another time, then," Lisa said, looking relieved.

"Right," agreed Stevie. "We can do it any old time."

10

CAROLE WAS SITTING in the tack room, giving her rider rating cards one final look. She had chosen the tack room because it was the only place in all of Pine Hollow that wasn't teeming with riders and activity. It was Saturday, the day of the show skills rally, and she had finished the first leg of her judging duties. She had spent the morning going from stall to stall, checking both ponies and riders on their appearance. How clean was the stall? How well groomed was the pony? Was the animal tacked up properly, and was the equipment being maintained properly? The results of her efforts were a small mountain of note cards, all of which she now needed to organize.

* * *

"HOLD STILL, JASMINE, or I'll end up sticking you in the throat," Lisa cautioned as she struggled to get the girl's stock pin absolutely straight.

Jasmine tapped her foot on the ground like a restless pony. "My dad is always saying he hates wearing ties, now I know why." She tried to run a finger around the inside of the high collar.

Lisa moved her hand away gently but firmly. "Stop that."

"But Carole already came by and inspected us, so what does it matter if my pin is a little crooked?"

It was true, that part of the judging was over. Lisa was very proud of the work Jasmine had put in, and while her braiding still left a lot to be desired, not even Carole could fault the girl on effort. Her pony's coat practically glowed, his tack was immaculate, and Jasmine's records were clear, precise, and up to the second. "You know Max is going to start the ring work soon. You don't want Outlaw to be ashamed of his rider, do you?" Lisa said, making a minuscule adjustment to the fine white linen. "There, that's perfect. You look like a pro." Lisa checked her watch. "Time to go."

Jasmine went pale. "I think I'm going to throw up," she said faintly.

Lisa grabbed her by the shoulders. "No, no, no. You're going to be fine. Take a deep breath."

She did as Lisa said.

"Now let it out slowly. Again." A little color came back into the girl's face. "Better?" Lisa asked.

Jasmine nodded and swallowed. "That was close."

"Don't worry about it," Lisa said, wrapping a protective arm around the girl's tiny shoulders. "I feel the same way practically every time I compete."

Jasmine was clearly surprised to hear that. "You do?"

Lisa steered her toward her pony's stall. "To tell you the truth, I think most riders feel that way before they go into the ring. Even the really experienced ones. Now, let's get out there and show everyone how good you and Outlaw really are."

FROM HER PLACE on the top rail of the ring, Stevie could take in every detail of Corey and Samurai's appearance, and she smiled with delight. Her concentration was broken, however, as, to her surprise, Lisa scrambled up to join her on her perch. Ever since they had canceled the sleepover in the hayloft there had been very little communication between the members of The Saddle Club.

Lisa settled herself comfortably on the rail. "Ribbons, huh?"

Stevie thought Lisa was making fun of her Pony Partner team and rose to their defense. "Corey has a real talent for braiding. It was her idea to weave green and black ribbons into Samurai's mane to match her riding jacket, and I think they look terrific."

"I have to admit, they are a nice touch. But ribbons don't win a horse race," Lisa declared firmly.

"And hoof black does?" Stevie asked, pointing to Jasmine's pony.

"What? There's nothing wrong with a little polish. I thought it might draw some attention to how well Outlaw picks up his feet over cavalletti," Lisa said defensively. "It does show off his white socks nicely, don't you think?"

They watched as Max put the young riders through their paces. He had started the class at the walk and then had them extend it. Everyone did fine. Next came a sitting trot. Stevie noticed that one rider, seven-year-old Liam, was having trouble keeping his balance. Corey, on the other hand, sat easily on her pony, the two of them completely in sync. Stevie felt like a proud parent.

"Posting trot, please, and riders change directions," Max instructed from the center of the ring.

"Oh! Did you see that?" Lisa said, nudging Stevie in

the ribs. "Jessica Adler circled Penny in an outside instead of an inside circle on the change of direction."

"Major mistake!" Stevie said. "I bet Andrea is about to tear her braids out."

"It was a silly mistake," Lisa agreed.

"Andrea should have prepared Jessica better."

Lisa nodded. "Absolutely."

The two of them grinned happily at each other.

The rest of the event consisted of collected and extended canters with changes of lead and direction. Jessica didn't make the same mistake again, but the damage was done. Stevie noticed that some of the riders were definitely more advanced than others, and she was gratified to see that Corey was one of them. Jasmine and May had also fared well.

Stevie hopped down from the rail. "Cavalletti are next, and I want to talk to Corey before her turn."

"I'll go with you," Lisa said. "There's something I want to say to Jasmine, too."

Stevie was eager to congratulate Corey on her fine performance and to make sure she stayed focused; the hardest part of the competition was still in front of them: first the cavalletti and then the final event, the jumping.

Corey, Jasmine, and May were standing next to each other, chatting excitedly. Stevie rushed up to her Pony

Partner and hugged her. "You are doing so well!" she told her warmly.

Corey returned her hug. "Thanks, Stevie. I tried to remember everything you told me."

Lisa slipped her arm around Jasmine. "And you are outstanding!"

"Wait until the cavalletti," Jasmine said seriously. "Outlaw is going to be perfect."

"I know you've worked hard on that, and no matter what happens today, I want you to know how proud I am of you," Lisa said.

Stevie noticed that all around them the other Pony Partner pairs were gathered in little groups, the younger riders getting congratulations and last-minute advice. The one exception was poor May, who, as usual, had no one in her corner. "Hey, May," she called, "you did a real nice job out there."

May smiled almost shyly. "Thanks, Stevie, but it's easy when you have a pony as good as Mac."

Stevie couldn't help wondering where Veronica was. Surely even she wouldn't be so selfish as to miss today's rally.

AS THE CAVALLETTI and jumps were being set up, Carole tried to shuffle her paperwork back into some kind of order. She was finding that sitting in judgment of her fellow riders was making her extremely uncomfortable. Every time one of the kids made a mistake, her instinct had been to offer advice, to help. Instead, she was forced to take away points. It made her feel bad.

Max strode up to her. "Ready, Madame Judge?" he said respectfully.

"Ready, Mr. Regnery," Carole replied. Addressing each other in a formal manner had been Max's idea. If she was going to have all the duties and pressures of being a judge, he said, she should have all the respect of one as well.

Together they made their way over to where a set of five cavalletti were set up. "Call the first rider, please, Mr. Regnery," Carole said.

In the cavalletti event, the riders began by showing their ponies at a walk, then at a posting trot, and finally at a canter with a very small jump at the end. Contestant after contestant paraded by and over the obstacles with varying degrees of success. Since change of gait necessitated an adjustment in the spacing of the poles, it was a time-consuming process, and Carole found herself struggling to remain focused on her job. She knew each individual deserved her full and undivided attention, but the truth was she was finding the whole process rather tedious.

The next contestant entered the ring. It was May

Grover on Macaroni. Carole watched as the girl carefully positioned her pony at the head of the cavalletti. When she was settled, Carole nodded for her to proceed. The entire routine was flawless and ended with the pair floating over the small jump at the end. They had made it all look easy. Still, Carole hesitated in jotting down their score. Something was wrong. She struggled to put her finger on the problem. She watched as the duo left the ring and suddenly knew what it was. With every other contestant's entrance and exit there had been at least one person whooping and shouting encouragement. For May there had been only a smattering of polite applause from her fellow riders. Where was May's cheerleader? Veronica diAngelo was nowhere around. Carole felt bad for the little girl, but there was nothing she could do about it. Corey Takamura had entered the ring and was waiting for her signal to start.

"DID YOU SEE that?" Stevie whooped, pounding on the railing. "Four jumps and a clear round!"

"Corey did rap that second one kind of hard, though," Lisa said.

Stevie turned to her. "It stayed up, didn't it? That's what wins a horse race," she said smugly.

"Maybe, but Carole's bound to take away points for

116

style. After all, Corey did have to grab a big handful of mane to stay on board," responded Lisa coolly.

Stevie turned back to the ring. "At least she didn't take down a pole, unlike some riders who shall remain nameless, but whose initials happen to be *J.J.*"

"Jasmine showed excellent form through the whole course," Lisa responded hotly. "A good seat and hands are the basis for a good rider, and at this stage of their training, that's equally as important as a clean round!"

"They both did a good job," Stevie conceded. "They should be proud of themselves."

"Let's go tell them," Lisa suggested.

Together they made their way through the small knots of people and ponies until they spotted Jasmine and Corey. There were hugs and congratulations all around. Both young riders were happy and flushed from the competition, and they seemed relieved that their part in the rally was over.

"You guys did great," May said enthusiastically. "I hope I can do as well."

"Hey, shouldn't you be mounting up?" Stevie asked.

"I guess so," May said, looking around. "I thought maybe Veronica . . ." She didn't finish the sentence. She didn't have to.

"Here, I'll give you a leg up," Stevie offered, moving to Macaroni's side and lacing her fingers together.

"Thanks, Stevie," May said gratefully. "I guess I'm as ready as I'll ever be."

Stevie eyed her equipment critically. "Not with those stirrups, you're not. May, you know you need them shorter for jumping," she gently scolded the girl as she made the adjustments.

"I guess I forgot," May apologized.

"That's not the only thing you've forgotten," Lisa said, stepping firmly in front of pony and rider.

The little girl looked puzzled.

"If you ride into the ring without your hat, Max'll have you riding back out so fast your head will spin."

"My hat! I don't know where I left it! What should I do?" she said, panicking.

"What size do you wear?" Lisa asked.

"A four," May said, her eyes starting to tear up.

Lisa looked at Jasmine and Corey, who both shook their heads regretfully. "Stay calm," she said, scanning the crowd of faces. "A-ha! I'll be right back." She disappeared into a small knot of people only to reappear a moment later with a hard hat clutched triumphantly in her hands. She presented her prize to May. "I borrowed this from Natalie, so don't forget to return it after the competition."

"You'd better get moving," Stevie advised.

May hesitated. "I'm not sure what the order of the course is."

Lisa was surprised. "Haven't you been watching the other riders?"

"Not as much as I should have, I guess," she confessed. "I wanted to make sure Mac looked his best."

"It's pretty simple, May," Stevie said. "Four fences set up in a square. You're going to be riding a figure eight. Jump the first one, cut through the middle and to the right, jump the second and loop to the left, over that and through the middle again to the last fence on your left," Stevie explained quickly.

"You'd better get going. I just heard them announce your name," Lisa told her. "Good luck."

As May rode off, Lisa, Stevie, Jasmine, and Corey all looked at each other with concern. Then they bolted for the fence to watch.

CAROLE WAS FEELING a profound sense of relief. A few more riders and it would all be over. She looked up in time to see May Grover bowing to her. She acknowledged the salute. A moment later the pony and rider were heading toward the first jump. The duo soared cleanly over the fence and headed for the second on the far side of the arena. Once again, May placed her pony in perfect jumping position, and they bounded over it.

It was as the pair made the loop toward the third fence that Carole spotted trouble. May overshot the next obstacle on the course and headed toward a much bigger one that had been stored to the right of the fence she was supposed to be jumping. Carole watched in helpless horror as Macaroni made his approach. May must have realized her error at the last moment. Carole saw her drop her hands, losing contact with her pony's mouth. The results were devastating. Macaroni, sensing his rider's loss of confidence, lost confidence himself. At the last possible moment he planted his forefeet in the ground and came to an abrupt stop. May, unprepared, went vaulting over her pony's head and landed on the far side of the jump in a heap.

Max ran to the fallen girl, Carole hot on his heels. Stevie, Lisa, and many of the other spectators arrived seconds later.

"Don't sit up, May," Max said, kneeling at her side. "Do you think you're hurt?"

"I don't know," the little girl said in a tearful voice.

"Try to move your arms and legs, one at a time," Max advised, watching her carefully.

Carole noticed that Macaroni was trotting around

the ring, trailing his reins and looking upset. "Stevie," she whispered. "Can you get her pony?"

Stevie nodded, moving off.

Carole watched closely as May gingerly tested her limbs. She thought the girl was going to get off with nothing more than injured pride until she moved her right wrist.

"Owww!" May yelped, clutching it with her other hand.

"Hurts to move it?" Max asked, concerned.

May nodded. Tears were beginning to roll down her dusty cheeks.

Max looked at Carole. "Help me get her up."

The two of them assisted the little girl slowly to her feet. She was obviously in some pain.

"I think we'd better get you to a doctor," Max said. "I'm going to run ahead and call your parents. Carole, can you walk her over to the stable to get her things?"

"Of course, Max," Carole answered at once.

As the two girls made their way slowly out of the arena, Stevie came back with Macaroni in tow. Somehow the pony managed to actually look embarrassed about the whole situation. "Thanks, Stevie." Carole took the animal's reins.

"Is there anything else I can do?" Stevie asked.

Carole considered a moment. "I doubt if Max will want to continue with the rally. Could you tell the others?"

"Of course," Stevie said right away. "I'm sorry you got hurt, May."

"Thanks, Stevie," the little girl sniffled.

"We'd better get going," Carole said.

The two girls made their way carefully to the stable. As Carole escorted May into the locker room, they discovered Veronica diAngelo sitting on one of the benches. Her lips were glistening from a freshly applied coat of gloss, and she held a cell phone to her ear.

"May, what are you doing in here?" Veronica demanded. "Shouldn't you be in the ring?"

"May is hurt," snapped Carole.

May gently held out her right wrist in her left hand. It was already swelling rapidly.

Veronica took one look at the wrist and wrinkled her nose. "Ewww. You should really have somebody look at that."

Carole had no patience for Veronica's insensitivity. "I put Macaroni in his stall, but someone needs to look after him," she said pointedly.

"It's not my pony," Veronica protested. "And this isn't my fault."

Carole threw her a furious look and Veronica seemed to get the message.

"Oh, all right," Veronica said grudgingly. "I don't suppose either of you has seen Red around?"

Carole didn't bother to reply.

ALL THE RIDERS were present when May's parents collected her for the short drive to the hospital. They were somber as they watched the Grovers' car disappear down the road. Although Pine Hollow had an excellent record and no rider there had ever been seriously injured, it was always upsetting when a rider got hurt at all, especially when it was someone as dedicated and careful as May.

They all looked to Max for some consolation, but he didn't have any for them. His face was stern, his eyes cold, and his lips were in a thin, straight line. He was angry and they knew it.

"I want you all to take care of your tack and your ponies and be in my office in five minutes. We have something to talk about. In fact, we have a lot to talk about."

"THIS IS A VERY sad day for Pine Hollow," Max began, his steely eyes glaring at everyone gathered in his office.

All around him, riders exchanged looks. Some of them were confused. Stevie knew what was on their minds: Accidents happen. They weren't fun for anybody, but they were accidents. How could Max be upset?

Stevie also knew that wasn't what Max was upset about.

He continued. "Most of you probably think I'm talking about May's fall. While there's no question that that is a sad event, what led up to it and what I see all around me now is tragic."

Again, the riders looked at one another, most still wondering what was up.

Mrs. Reg knocked on the door and gestured to Max. He left the riders alone and confused for a few minutes.

Carole listened silently as whispers broke out in the office. She knew what was coming. The whispers weren't intended for her ears, but the room was small and the messages were clear.

"How could Carole tell how clean his coat was when you practically needed a Seeing Eye dog to get in his stall?" Brittany Lynn hissed to her friend, Polly, sitting two feet away. "We are talking zero light in there! It's all her fault."

Stevie turned to Lisa. "You realize of course that we now have no chance of winning this thing, don't you?" she asked.

"Why do you say that?" Lisa asked.

"Come on, Lisa. Carole never tried to hide the fact that May was her favorite. Now with the accident, she's also got the sympathy vote.

Lisa looked at the floor and said nothing.

"Well," said Betsy in another corner, leaning over to Meg. "If Natalie doesn't care about winning, it's no skin off my nose. I'm sure not going to do all the work for her!"

125

Reuben turned to Mark, sitting behind him. "I could buff that old saddle until my fingers bleed and it's still never going to look as good as Leslie's new one. So what's the point in even trying?"

Carole listened to the riders around her, each one totally focused on themselves, and began to have an inkling of what was really bothering Max. She realized, too, that this griping had been going on for more than a week. It wasn't always this loud or this furious, but it was always there. The only reason it was all hanging out now was because everyone was so upset about May. But the mood had been there all along. For the first time, it occurred to her to wonder what part she'd played in setting that mood.

Max returned, glaring at the unhappy chatter that surrounded him.

"That was May's father calling to say they were at the hospital and May is being examined," Max said. "Now, where was I? Yes, how could I forget. My original purpose was to give young riders confidence, garnered from the experience of the older ones—confidence in your growing abilities, confidence in the reliability of your mounts, and confidence in the unfailing support of your fellow riders. When I learned that some of the older riders thought their job was to watch, not teach, I thought, well, they'll learn. When

I heard some riders trashing others, I thought, well, they'll find out that they do better when they help one another than when they put others down. When I saw that the only thing that mattered to some of the riders was winning ribbons, I thought, gee, I thought I'd taught them better than that! And when I saw friend-ships bruised because of some kind of presumed fa-voritism, I thought, oh no. There are so many things so much more important. When will they learn?"

He paused and looked around the room, his eye catching the eye of every single rider in there so that each and every one of them knew he meant them— not someone else.

"But you haven't learned, you haven't changed, you haven't grown. The bickering I just walked in on is proof of that. I am truly saddened to say that every-thing I see now tells me this whole exercise was a failure!"

There was a slight murmur of protest from a few peo-ple in the room, but as Carole looked around, she could tell that most of the group seemed to feel that a guilty silence was a more honest response. Stevie dared to peek around her, only to find almost everybody had developed a sudden fascination with their own foot-gear.

"How many times have I told you that the only per-

son you're competing against is yourself? The only reason to compete at all is to inspire and challenge yourself to grow. You should be taking delight in each
other's achievements, cheering each other along, not
complaining and cutting your fellow riders down. In
fact, the only sincere case of good sportsmanship I've
seen in some time was when two of you made the effort to find a helmet to replace May's missing one."
Stevie felt good for a tiny second, until Max continued. "A nice thing to do, but sadly that may have been
the only action of its kind this week."

Again Max paused, looking at everyone. It was small
consolation to Lisa and Stevie, but they knew he
wasn't just angry at them. He was angry at everyone.

"We are suspending this competition for today. I
don't know what I want to do about tomorrow or about
the full Pony Club rally. At the moment, I'm too upset
to make a rational decision."

"But, Max, we put in so much work!" Veronica
protested.

Stevie's mouth fell open. She turned to make sure it
was actually Veronica who had uttered those words.
It was.

"I can't believe she said that," Stevie gasped to Lisa.

"And here I thought nothing she ever did or said

again could surprise me," Lisa said, shaking her head in wonder.

"I am well aware of the amount and the caliber of work each and every one of you has put in," Max said to Veronica.

Veronica squirmed under his gaze.

"Nonetheless, until I see a marked change in the behavior and attitude around here, we will not be going forward with this rally. I want you all to go home and give some serious thought to what it is you expect to get out of riding. If you're only in it for the trophies and blue ribbons, you have no business being at this stable." Max scooped a piece of paper off his desk. "Carole, I want to thank you for all your hard work these last couple of weeks. I believe this belongs to you." He held out the paper.

Carole took it from him and examined it. "Max, this is a copy of the judging criteria. You already gave it to me." She offered it back.

"Actually that *is* the one I gave you. I needed to make some copies for myself so I borrowed it from your cubby a while back. I should have mentioned it to you sooner, but it slipped my mind. I apologize.

"Anyway," Max continued, "you don't seem to have missed it, so no harm done. Whether you'll still be needing it remains to be seen. That said"—he turned back to the class—"we will all meet again tomorrow morning to see if any one of you can come up with a good reason for us to continue with the meet." He walked out of the room. Slowly everyone began to file out.

Carole remained standing by Max's desk. She was staring at the paper in her hands, her face a war of emotions.

Stevie was about to suggest to Lisa that they go and see what was going on when Lisa bolted out of the room. "Lisa?" she called after the fleeing figure. She stood there, torn. Should she follow Lisa or should she go over to Carole? She decided to talk to Carole first, and then the two of them could go after Lisa. She approached her friend. "Is something wrong, Carole? You look kind of funny."

"Oh, Stevie, I've done something terrible!" she exclaimed.

The stricken look on her friend's face caught Stevie off guard. "What?"

"I've betrayed a friendship," Carole replied, looking sadly at the door Lisa had disappeared through.

"What do you mean?"

Carole quickly filled Stevie in on what had been happening between her and Lisa over the last week:

her suspicions, catching Lisa in the act, and how badly she had been treating her since then.

Stevie was shocked. "I can't believe I didn't notice things weren't right between you two."

"You've had other things on your mind," Carole replied. "I expect Lisa has told Max all about it by now. Some judge I turned out to be, huh?" she said, hanging her head.

Stevie didn't know how to console Carole. Lisa certainly had every right to be angry, and no one could blame her if she complained to Max about Carole's behavior.

Carole sighed deeply. "I guess I'd better go find him and face the music," she said glumly. "Not to mention apologizing to Lisa. I have no idea how I'm going to make this up to her!"

"How about starting with a sleepover in the loft tonight?" Lisa asked, appearing in the doorway. "I just cleared it with Max."

12

SATURDAY EVENING FOUND the three girls holding their first Saddle Club meeting in weeks. Lisa hadn't complained to Max about Carole at all. Figuring that the three of them needed some time alone to set things right between them, she had asked him if they could have their sleepover in the loft after all. Now they were sitting in a semicircle on their sleeping bags, armed only with sodas, chips, and very bruised feelings.

"I can't believe you guys didn't tell me what was going on," Stevie complained.

"I did tell you," Carole said quietly.

"Oh sure, about five minutes ago," Stevie grumped,

reaching for another potato chip from the bag at her feet.

Lisa smiled. "As usual you're exaggerating. It was closer to five hours ago. Chips please."

"Whatever. The point is, one of you should have at least mentioned it."

"Actually," Carole said, "I think the point is that none of it should have been going on in the first place." She looked sadly at Lisa. "I still don't know how I could have thought you would do something like that, Lisa. You're one of the most honorable people I've ever met." She hung her head.

"Carole, stop! You've already apologized twenty times and I've accepted." Lisa took a sip of her soda before trying to put her feelings into words. "It hurt a lot that you thought I could do something like that, but what made it worse was that I couldn't think of how to prove my innocence to you."

Carole shook her head. "You shouldn't have had to prove anything to me. I was supposed to be your friend."

Watching Carole struggle to come to terms with what she had done over the last week, Lisa couldn't help thinking that it was often easier to forgive someone else than it was to forgive yourself. She leaned across the space between them. "I've got news for you. You *are* my friend." She held out the bag. "Chip?"

Carole took a big handful and smiled for what might have been the first time in weeks.

"Speaking of proving something," Stevie said, leaning back on her elbows and eyeing Carole. "Why have you been so hard on Corey and me? Did we do something to make you mad?"

Carole looked surprised. "No!" She thought a moment. "Well, to tell you the truth, I did think you should have been teaching her better organizational skills, but other than that I don't think I've treated you any differently than the others."

"You're kidding, right?" Stevie said incredulously.

Carole looked defensive. "Actually, I'm not."

"I don't know about Lisa, but you've been twice as hard on me and Corey as you have been on everybody else." She saw the doubt on Carole's face. "Remember the day you patted Samurai on the flank and he was dusty?"

Carole nodded.

"That same day Natalie's horse had been so badly groomed that he had mud crusted on his belly."

"That's true," Carole confirmed.

"I would be real curious to see what you wrote in

your notes about the two things," Stevie challenged her.

"I'm not sure I should be doing this, but for the sake of fairness . . ." Carole took out her judge's folder and thumbed through a few pages. *"Corey's pony was filthy today,"* she read from her notes. *"Extremely lazy grooming habits."*

"Now read us what you wrote about Natalie that day," Lisa urged.

Carole flipped a few more pages. *"Natalie's pony had a trace of mud on his belly. Probably an accidental oversight."* She closed the folder.

" 'Filthy' with 'lazy grooming habits,' versus 'accidental oversight,' " Stevie said. "You still think you weren't being overly harsh on us?"

"I have to admit, in that instance I might have overstepped a little with you," Carole acknowledged. "But I'm sure it was only that one time."

"Carole, I'm sorry, but I really have to side with Stevie on this," Lisa said as gently as she could. This might not have been the best time to hash all this out, but she felt she had as much of an obligation to stand up for Jasmine as Stevie did for Corey.

"You too, Lisa?" Carole asked. "Are you sure you don't feel that way because of what was happening between us?"

135

Stevie sat up. "Yeah, Lisa, as far as I could tell, Carole was bending over backward to help you and Jasmine every time you asked."

Lisa was completely surprised. "What are you talking about?"

"When I went to make that phone call in Mrs. Reg's office, I came out and Carole was helping you with cavalletti." She looked at her friends accusingly. "I don't know what training secrets she shared with you, but it didn't seem fair to the rest of us."

Lisa and Carole exchanged looks. "What you saw, Stevie, was Carole giving me the brush-off," Lisa explained. "I did ask for advice that day, and she told me that until the meet was over I was on my own, like everybody else." She turned to Carole. "By the way, I think you were right."

Carole looked grateful. "For what it's worth, I never doubted you would figure out what to tell Jasmine, and you did. You just needed to have confidence in your own teaching abilities."

"So all this time you weren't helping her?" Stevie asked.

"Helping me? I thought she was helping you!" Lisa confessed. "When you guys stopped calling me, I figured you were talking to each other, about me and about . . . stuff." Now that she'd said it aloud it sounded even more ridiculous than it had in her head all those weeks. "But Carole, I really do think you were being harder on our two Pony Partners than on the rest of the group."

"Look, you two, I'm a judge. I have to be hard."

"Hard, yes—" Stevie agreed.

"But equally hard on everybody," Lisa finished.

Carole looked at them both. "You two are saying I've been harder on both of you?"

The girls nodded in unison.

"Tell you what," she said, putting her folder on the floor in front of her. "Give me some specific instances and I'll check them out. That way we can settle this, one way or the other. Okay?"

Again Lisa and Stevie nodded their consent. For the next fifteen minutes they rattled off incidents where they felt they had been punished for being Carole's friends. Carole checked out each of the complaints in her folder. Lisa and Stevie were surprised a few times to find out Carole had been just as strict with other competitors as she had been with them. However, when they were finished, Carole had to admit there were many more instances when she had definitely come down harder on her friends.

"It looks like I owe you both an apology," Carole said, closing the record book. "I guess I didn't realize how paranoid Veronica diAngelo's comment must have made me."

"You're only human," Lisa consoled her.

"That's more than anybody can say about Veronica," Stevie cracked.

Lisa and Carole laughed.

"You know, Max is right," Lisa said suddenly. "Riding shouldn't be about the ribbons and trophies, it should be about this." She indicated Stevie and Carol. "It should be about friendship."

"And horses," added Stevie.

"I feel so much better now," Carole said, smiling. "I can't tell you how much I've missed talking to you guys."

"Why didn't you pick up the phone and call us?" Lisa asked. "Before the thing with your notes I mean," she added hastily.

Carole smacked the folder on the floor in front of her. "It was this . . . thing!" she cried in frustration. "I felt in order to be absolutely impartial, I couldn't tell anyone what I was thinking or how overwhelmed I was feeling."

Stevie looked surprised. "But Carole, we were the ones under pressure to be perfect. You only had to choose who was doing it better."

"Do you have any idea how hard it is to decide who,

out of all the riders here, does the best job picking a hoof clean?" she moaned. "I felt terrible taking off points for mistakes that normally wouldn't mean a thing." She threw herself flat on her sleeping bag. "And everybody hates me!" she howled.

Stevie turned to Lisa. "Did you know she could be this melodramatic?"

Lisa considered Carole writhing on her bag. "No, I have to say this is a new side to her. She's almost as good as you."

"Carole, don't be dense," Stevie chided her. "You're going to be a hero around here. Don't you know that?"

Carole sat up. "What do you mean?"

"She means," Lisa said, taking over, "our team is almost certain to take every prize at that under-twelve pony rally, thanks mostly to your being such an irritating, nitpicky perfectionist."

"She's right," Stevie assured her. "They may want to burn you at the stake today, but a couple of weeks from now they'll be carrying your ashes in a parade."

"It's true," added Lisa.

"You really think so?" asked Carole.

"Absolutely," Stevie assured her.

"It's really too bad Max canceled our rally," Lisa said wistfully. "Even though we were all pretty bad sportsmen, we did get a lot of other things accomplished."

Stevie eyed Carole. "I have to admit, it would have been interesting to see who you would have picked."

"I guess we'll never know," Carole said, slipping into her sleeping bag. "At least now the pressure is off." She sighed, putting her head down on her soft pillow.

"Maybe for you," Stevie replied, thumping her own pillow with obvious annoyance. "For me it's only getting worse by the hour!"

"The anniversary thing?" Lisa asked as she settled herself in for sleep.

Stevie moaned. "How can my brothers and I possibly show our parents how much we love them when we can't even work together long enough to come up with a present?"

Carole rolled onto her side and propped her chin in her hand. "Don't worry, Stevie. Present or not, your parents know you love them. You show them every day."

"Sure," Lisa said from the snugly warmth of her own sleeping bag. "Like they say, some of the best presents don't come with wrapping paper."

For the first time in many days, all the members of The Saddle Club fell asleep with smiles on their faces.

CAROLE RAN THE soft cloth gently down Starlight's nose, taking special care to make sure the lopsided white star on his forehead was clean. Suddenly the horse began to rub his face on her chest. "Hey," she laughed, bracing herself. "Did I tickle you?" Starlight continued using her as a scratching post for a few more seconds before backing off. Carole looked down at the front of her shirt, which now had little horsehairs stuck all over it. "Thanks a lot," she said. "Now I have to change before the meeting." Starlight regarded her so solemnly she couldn't resist throwing her arms around his neck. "I don't care what Chad Lake says," she whispered, breathing in his warm, horsey scent. "I love the way you smell."

"Can I interrupt, or do the two of you want to be alone?" Stevie said, standing in the aisle outside the stall.

"Do you have an appointment?" Carole asked, glancing with fake haughtiness over her shoulder.

Stevie leaned on the stall door. "No, but I do know the girl who shovels the manure around here. Will that get me a hearing?"

Carole addressed the horse. "What do you think, Starlight, should we grant her an audience?"

"Enjoy your days in power while you can, Madame Judge; they may be coming to a quick end," Stevie warned her. "I just saw Max going into his office."

"Oh gosh," Carole cried, letting go of Starlight and slipping out of the stall. "I've got to change my shirt." She hurried toward the locker room. "Hey, where's Lisa?"

"Oh, I think she's in the locker room guarding your judging file," Stevie said casually, tagging along.

Carole threw her a dirty look. "That is *so* funny I forgot to laugh. Have you ever considered going professional?"

Stevie looked hurt. "What makes you think I'm not?"

"Your jokes," Carole replied emphatically.

As it turned out, Lisa *was* in the locker room, along

142

with half a dozen other people getting ready for class. Everyone seemed to be speculating about what Max planned to tell them. Carole put on a clean shirt and kept quiet. She already knew what she was going to say when she got to the meeting. She hadn't told Stevie or Lisa yet because she knew they would try to talk her out of it, and she couldn't let them do that.

Lisa came over to her. "All set?"

Carole grabbed her judging folder. "Lead on."

As the three of them made their way to Max's office, Carole had a sudden inspiration. "Remember when I asked you guys to go on a trail ride with me, and you said you couldn't?"

Stevie and Lisa nodded.

"Well, if Max is going to cancel the rally, why don't we go on one today?"

"That's a great idea," said Lisa.

"We might as well, since we're already here," Stevie conceded happily.

The three of them trooped in to Max's office. Since they were among the last to arrive, they had to stand at the back.

Max started the meeting. "First off I should tell you that I got a call from May's parents this morning. It turns out she broke her wrist." Everyone grew solemn at this bit of news. "It was a greenstick fracture," he continued, "which means she'll be out of her cast in a few weeks."

Carole, who had grown particularly fond of the little girl, was saddened to hear the news. She knew from the time she had spent with Judy Barker, the Pine Hollow vet, that a greenstick fracture was like a crack in a bone instead of an outright break. Judy had shown her what one looked like by stripping a small living branch off a tree and bending it practically in two. Because it was so fresh, the little twig had split instead of snapping apart.

Max looked serious. "I hope you all took some time last night to think over what I said."

Several heads around the room bobbed, acknowledging that they had done so.

"Well, so have I. I no longer think that we should postpone our rally."

There were murmurs of surprise and delight throughout the room.

Max held up his hands for silence. "All things considered, I feel it might be in everyone's best interest to cancel the rally altogether."

Max was peppered with protests from practically every corner.

Stevie stepped forward. "Maybe he's right," she said

loudly. Everyone focused on her. "Look. We have to admit we kind of blew it. Our attitude toward each other has become more about winning than about learning and teaching. Especially mine," she confessed. "I'm not saying we all haven't gotten a lot of good things out of this, it's just that good sportsmanship wasn't one of them." The younger kids looked glum and the older ones guilty. "I think maybe we should salvage what we can from the experience and move on."

Jessica looked like she was going to cry. "But we worked so hard."

"We weren't all bad," Leslie protested.

Natalie nodded, her little face already getting blotchy from unshed tears. "Couldn't we just try harder?" she asked in a quavering voice.

Carole decided it was time for her to say something. "Excuse me."

"Yes, Carole? Do you have something to add?" Max asked.

Carole cleared her throat. "Yes, I guess I do." She looked at the small sea of sad faces. This was going to be hard, but she knew she had to say it. "I have a confession to make. The problems with the rally weren't being made by only you guys. I was making them, too.

I tried my best to be fair and impartial, and I failed." She found she didn't want to look anyone in the face.

"How is that?" Max prodded gently.

Carole took a deep breath. "I know for a fact that I was unjustly hard on some people and unreasonably easy on others. The problem is that it doesn't seem fair of me to try to choose a winner when all around me I keep seeing people trying their best. Because that's what I think is really important: trying your best." She met Max's eyes. "If that makes me a bad judge, then I understand if you want to replace me."

"Replace you?" Max smiled. "It's that very attitude that makes you such a fine choice."

Carole could hardly believe it. She had expected to be completely humiliated by confessing her failure, and now she was being congratulated instead.

Max rubbed his hands together. "I think we're finally making some progress here. I'm gratified to see this improvement in your attitudes. In fact, I am so pleased that I've decided we will finish up our rally today after all."

With that announcement the room descended into chattering chaos. Some kids were delighted, others reluctant.

When the room had calmed down a bit, Max resumed speaking. "Many of you had already completed your final event before we were interrupted by May's accident yesterday. Nonetheless, I want all the contestants to saddle up your ponies and put on your show outfits. We will meet in the ring for the end of the jumping event as soon as you can get ready."

Class was excused and everyone scattered in different directions, frantic to get ready.

"I guess that kind of puts a damper on our trail ride," Lisa said wistfully.

"Not necessarily," Carole said. "The jumping event won't take long. We can go right after."

"I'm afraid we're going to be too busy right after," Stevie told her.

"Doing what?" Carole asked.

"Attending your funeral," Stevie crowed, grinning. " 'Cause all the losers are going to kill you!"

Lisa sidled closer to Carole. "By the way, nice try back there at getting off the hook, but . . ." She swatted her on the back. "Tag, you're still it!"

Lisa and Stevie sprinted away, laughing.

ONCE AGAIN CAROLE found herself standing in the center of the ring, judging the young riders as they tried their hand over the small jumps. Today, however, she was finding the experience much more to her liking. She was still anxious about having to choose the winner, but knowing that Max had complete confidence in her gave her confidence in herself.

Before the event began, the larger jumps were turned against the outer railing in order to avoid any possibility of another accident like May's.

There was also another difference: the attitude of the people watching. A loud cheer and a hearty round of applause greeted each and every rider as they entered and exited the arena, regardless of how they had performed. Consolation and suggestions were offered to those who had a rough time of it, and heartfelt congratulations were handed out to the more successful.

After the final rider had completed the event, Carole was left alone in Max's office to figure out the winner of the rally. When she eventually emerged, she found all the riders mounted on their ponies and waiting for her in the ring. Max ordered them all into a tidy line, like a ribbon presentation in a real show.

Taking a deep breath, Carole entered the ring, raised her chin, and strode forward with all the authority she could muster. Max gave her a little bow, which she acknowledged with a regal nod of her head. Then she addressed the riders. "First of all, I would like to congratulate each and every one of you for all the hard work you have put in for the past two weeks. You have all made great progress and have every right to be proud of yourselves."

The young riders beamed with pleasure at her praise.

"However," she continued, "you have made it impossible for me to do the job I was assigned."

The line of riders in front of her looked confused and disappointed.

Carole opened her folder. "My problem is this: I've been asked to give out one prize to an overall winner, but many of you are deserving of individual prizes. Reuben, for instance, kept his pony's stall immaculate at all times. Jasmine's records were flawless . . . as was her penmanship," she added, winking at the girl. "Corey is so good at braiding she could practically rent her services out, and I've never seen a more consistently or better groomed pony than Jessica's. You all deserve your own first prize." Carole lowered her list and looked at the row of competitors. "According to the rules, I'm supposed to select one of you as our champion, but after thinking it over, I've come to the conclusion that *you* are the ones who should be making that decision." From the corner of her eye, Carole could see Max watching her curiously.

"What did you have in mind, Madame Judge?" he asked.

"Could I have all the senior Pony Partners come out

149

here?" she called, waving at them where they were leaning on the fence, listening. When they were gathered around her, she explained. "As much as I've been observing you all over the last two weeks, it occurred to me that you have all been watching each other equally as closely." She saw rueful smiles. "So I think each of you knows who he or she thinks really deserves this prize. That's why I am giving everyone a vote. I'm going to come over to each of you now and let you tell me who you think is the most deserving."

Carole approached the first rider. "What do you say, Liam? Who should get the ribbon?"

"May Grover," he said without hesitation.

"But she didn't finish the competition," Carole said carefully.

"She didn't have anyone to teach her the course," he replied solemnly.

"She didn't have anyone to teach her at all!" declared Corey, who was next to him.

Her statement was greeted by a chorus of agreement from almost all the other riders.

"I bet if she hadn't broken her wrist, she would have gotten back on Mac and finished," someone else called.

It didn't take long for Carole to make her way down the line, but by the time she was halfway through, the winner was already clear. She returned to her place at the center of the group. "It is with the greatest pleasure that I tell you that the winner, by a nearly unanimous decision, is May Grover on Macaroni."

Everyone cheered, unsettling some of the ponies.

"I bow to the wisdom of our judge," Max said, "and to the decision of the majority. May has shown a lot of heart and determination," he conceded. "It's traditional for the winner to take a victory gallop around the ring. Since May isn't here to do it herself, maybe her friends would like to take it for her?" he suggested to the mounted riders.

Everyone let out another whoop.

Carole watched happily as the small herd of ponies and riders pounded around the ring. She felt the tension of the last few weeks draining from her body. Her job here, finally, was done.

After the victory lap all the young Pony Partners were excused. The older ones made themselves useful to Max by resetting the larger jumps in their normal positions, without being asked to do so.

"It seems a shame May couldn't have been here to collect her ribbon in person," Stevie said to Carole as they struggled to maneuver an obstacle back into its place.

"I know what you mean," Carole agreed. "There's

nothing quite like the moment when you win your first ribbon. Actually I did talk to Max about that, and he said that at the very next meeting May is able to attend, we could do a little presentation ceremony for her."

Stevie eyed the position of the jump critically. "Do you think Veronica will actually grace us with her presence on that day?"

"I don't think anyone will miss her if she doesn't," Carole replied, giving her end of the jump a final nudge.

Stevie gave a wicked smile. "Kind of like today?"

Carole spotted Lisa across the ring and waved her over. "I have to say, it doesn't surprise me much that she didn't show up. I'm sure she figured May was out of the running, so why should she bother?"

Stevie rolled her eyes in disgust. "She barely bothered showing up when she thought May *was* in the running!"

Lisa caught up with them as they were heading through the gate. "Let me guess," she said. "You two are talking about either the anniversary present or Veronica diAngelo."

"It was Veronica," Carole confirmed. "How did you know?"

"That's easy. Stevie looks like she ate a lemon."

Stevie frowned. "I can't help it. Even the sound of her name makes my hair stand on end."

"I have to admit, it's much more pleasant when she's not around," Lisa said. "Did I ever tell you what she and Betsy said to Carole in TD's?"

"No, but I bet it was something mean." Stevie sighed. "Veronica is unpleasant enough when she's here at Pine Hollow," she said, recalling the incident outside the ice cream shop. "But she's even worse when she's away from it! I should know."

The three girls entered the stable and were greeted by the sounds of happy, chattering riders.

Carole stopped in the doorway. "Listen to that. Isn't it so much more pleasant than all that squawking from last week?"

"Absolutely," Lisa agreed. "Still, nice as it is, what I could really use is some peace and quiet."

"Trail ride?" Carole said eagerly.

"Trail ride," Lisa confirmed.

Stevie stood stock-still. Something was coming together in her head and she didn't want to disturb it until it was complete.

"Stevie? Are you okay?" Lisa asked.

"Yes!" she shouted. "Yes, yes, yes!" Her two friends

were looking at her like she had lost her mind. But she didn't care. She had finally figured out the answer to her problem.

"Yes, you're okay, or yes, you want to go on a trail ride?" Carole asked, eyeing her doubtfully.

Stevie was jubilant. "Both!" she cried. "Look, do me a favor and saddle Belle for me. I'll meet you two outside." She started to hurry away.

"Stevie, where are you going?" Lisa called after her.

"To make a phone call," she answered.

Carole started to protest. "But Mrs. Reg won't—"

Stevie stopped and faced them, grinning from ear to ear. "It's an emergency!" she shouted joyfully.

14

STEVIE SAVORED THE dappled sunlight on her face and took a deep breath of fresh air. Beneath her, Belle moved eagerly and surely along the familiar trail that would take the three riders to Willow Creek.

"Doesn't it feel like forever since we've been on a trail ride?" Lisa asked from her position behind Stevie.

"I know what you mean," Stevie said, speaking over her shoulder. "I love our riding classes with Max, but sometimes I think I love this even more."

Carole, who had been trailing the other two, urged Starlight up alongside Lisa. "I can't believe we haven't been out here for two weeks," she said. "What were we thinking of?"

Lisa smiled ruefully. "Pony Partners."

"Judging duties," Carole admitted.

"Anniversary presents," Stevie finished.

"That reminds me," Carole said, "aren't you going to let us in on this mysterious phone call of yours back at the stable?"

"I can't believe Mrs. Reg actually let you use the phone again," Lisa teased.

Stevie smiled triumphantly. "Well, she did. As for the rest of it, you two are going to have to wait until we get to the creek. Right now Belle wants to canter."

Stevie nudged her horse with her heels. That was all the encouragement Belle needed. With a snort, she bounded forward, seemingly as eager as her rider to feel the wind in her face. Stevie sat easily in the saddle, keeping an eye out for low-hanging branches and relishing the rhythmic rocking of her mount. She could hear the pounding of Lisa's and Carole's horses as they followed.

All too soon they approached the turnoff that would lead them down to the water, and Stevie reluctantly reined Belle to a halt. She waited as the others brought their horses to a stop next to her.

"Gosh, that felt good," Lisa gushed.

Carole was smiling. "I think the horses enjoy that as much as we do."

"Let's get off and walk them the rest of the way,"

Stevie suggested. They all dismounted and she led them down the slope, picking her way carefully so that there would be no danger of the horses slipping.

Once they had reached their favorite spot, the three girls removed their horses' bridles and slipped on the halters they had brought with them. Then they tied the long lead ropes to the nearby trees so that the animals would be free to graze while the girls soaked their feet in the stream.

"Carole, could you help me?" Stevie asked, struggling to remove her footgear. English riding boots were notoriously difficult to remove without a bootjack.

Carole did the honors, helping both Stevie and Lisa, and they, in turn, pulled off hers. The whole thing nearly ended up with Lisa falling in the creek when Carole's boot came off more suddenly than expected. Luckily she managed to catch her balance in time. Laughing, the three of them settled down on the bank to dangle their toes in the cool water and chat. Inevitably, the subject of the pony rally came up.

"So, Carole, when did you come up with the idea of letting everyone vote on the winner?" Lisa wanted to know.

"Not until I was sitting in Max's office reviewing all my notes."

"Phew, you cut that close," Stevie observed.

"It was a stroke of genius, if I do say so myself," said Carole, pretending to be self-satisfied.

"More like the last act of a desperate woman," Stevie said, kicking water at her. "But I have to admit, it was the perfect solution."

"And the fairest," Lisa added warmly. "Max said you have all the qualities that make a good judge. Would you ever consider doing that as a career?"

"Not a chance!" Carole replied emphatically. She started to giggle. "I guess I'm just a Cobweb after all."

"Huh?" said two voices at once.

Carole told them about Mrs. Reg's story.

"I wonder why Mrs. Reg never comes right out and tells you what she wants you to know?" Stevie asked, puzzled.

"I think she'd tell you it's not her nature. Like it wasn't Cobweb's to like pulling carts or mine to enjoy judging others."

"And how it *is* Veronica's nature to be useless," Lisa added.

Stevie threw a small pebble into the lazy creek and watched the ripples spread. "It turns out Veronica isn't completely useless, Lisa." She enjoyed her friends' incredulous stares. "Well, she did help me come up with the perfect present for my parents' anniversary. In fact, all three of you did." She rolled casually onto her stomach.

"Lisa, me, and *Veronica?*" Carole asked doubtfully. Stevie nodded.

Lisa frowned. "I don't remember making any suggestions. Do you, Carole?"

Carole shook her head. "Not me, and I certainly can't picture Veronica offering anything if she thought it would be helpful to Stevie."

Stevie sat up abruptly. "That's just it. She didn't know she was being helpful. Veronica told me the best thing my brothers and I could do would be to run away with the circus."

Carole was clearly horrified. "Stevie, you're not seriously considering that, are you?"

Stevie laughed. "Of course not. What Veronica was implying was that things would be more peaceful around our house for my parents if my brothers and I weren't around."

"I hope you realize your mom and dad would never trade one moment of being with you guys for a lifetime of quiet," Lisa said solemnly.

Stevie smiled wryly. "Well, I don't know, they might like *one* moment. Anyway, last night before we went to sleep, Lisa said, 'Some of the best presents don't come with wrapping paper,' remember?"

Lisa shrugged. "So?"

"And then a little while ago as we all came into the stable after the rally, Carole made the comment about how nice it was to hear laughter after all the squabbling of the last couple of weeks."

"Did I?"

"Something like that, anyway. So you see? Between Veronica and you guys, that's where I got the idea for the present!" she finished.

"No, we don't see!" cried Lisa.

"Oh," Stevie said casually.

Carole started to tickle her. "What's the present?"

"Tell us!" Lisa pounced, joining in.

"Okay, okay!" Stevie gasped between giggles. "Uncle!" Her friends relented. "The present is the reason I had to go make that phone call. I needed to clear it with my brothers first. We've all agreed. Starting today there will be no arguments, practical jokes, or name-calling for an entire week." She looked at her two friends. "In other words, we're giving my parents exactly what they asked us for when you guys spent the night two weeks ago," she said triumphantly. "Peace and quiet!"

"Stevie, you've done it again," Lisa said, shaking her head in wonder.

Carole looked skeptical. "It's a great idea, but do you think you and your brothers can actually do it?"

"It won't be so hard," Stevie assured them. "A couple of sleepovers at your house, Carole . . . a few dinners at Lisa's . . . avoiding my brothers at all costs . . ."

"Sounds like a Saddle Club project to me," Carole said to Lisa.

Lisa nodded. "Maybe the hardest one yet!" she replied.

"Awww, come on, guys," Stevie coaxed. "The time's gonna fly. Trust me!"

ABOUT THE AUTHOR

BONNIE BRYANT is the author of more than a hundred books about horses, including The Saddle Club series, The Saddle Club Super Editions, the Pony Tails series, and Pine Hollow, which follows the Saddle Club girls into their teens. She has also written novels and movie novelizations under her married name, B. B. Hiller.

Ms. Bryant began writing The Saddle Club in 1986. Although she had done some riding before that, she intensified her studies then and found herself learning right along with her characters Stevie, Carole, and Lisa. She claims that they are all much better riders than she is.

Ms. Bryant was born and raised in New York City. She still lives there, in Greenwich Village, with her two sons.

Don't miss the next exciting
Saddle Club adventure . . .

NEW RIDER
Saddle Club #96

Zachary Simpson has only just started riding at Pine
Hollow, but everyone is totally impressed by his natural talent. Everyone except Carole Hanson, that is.
She's glad that he seems to love riding, but she's a little uncomfortable with the amount of attention he's
getting from everyone else in Pony Club. Is Carole just
jealous? And is Zach a mere flash in the pan, or is he
the real thing? The upcoming Pony Club competition
should give Zach a chance to show everyone what he's
capable of and to answer those questions.

But Zach falls apart, and the show is a disaster. Then
he announces that he's going to quit riding. Suddenly
it's up to Carole to remind Zach of all the things that
make riding and horses so special. Can she persuade
him to get back in the saddle?

MEET
the SADDLE CLUB

Horse lover CAROLE . . .
Practical joker STEVIE . . .
Straight-A LISA . . .

THE SADDLE CLUB SUPER EDITIONS

THE SADDLE CLUB SPECIAL EDITIONS

PINE HOLLOW

by Bonnie Bryant

*B*est friends Stevie, Carole, and Lisa have always stuck together. But everything has changed now that they're in high school. They've got boyfriends, jobs, and serious questions that they must grapple with on their own.

More and more they're discovering that sometimes even the best of friends can't solve your most serious problems.

Does this change in their lives mark the end of everything, or a brand-new beginning?

BFYR 240

Bantam